The Midnight Years

Jane De Suza's books have hit award and bestselling lists. These include *Flyaway Boy*, *When the World Went Dark*, the *SuperZero* series, *Uncool, Happily Never After* and *The Spy who Lost her Head,* among others. She is a management graduate from XLRI, was creative director across advertising agencies, is a columnist with a national daily, and currently lives in Singapore with her family.

Sangita Unni is a psychologist who lives in Bengaluru, and has been a practising counsellor for over a decade. She was the director of Lyftly India, and in 2020 launched Lyftly Minds, an app that promotes holistic emotional wellness, focused on the youth of our country. She is an avid trekker, diver, founder of Nair's Kitchen, and full-time mother to her three young-adult sons and beautiful indie dog.

The Midnight Years

Jane De Suza * Sangita Unni

hachette
INDIA

First published in 2021 by Hachette India
(Registered name: Hachette Book Publishing India Pvt. Ltd)
An Hachette UK company
www.hachetteindia.com

1

ISBN 978-81-947153-0-6

Hachette Book Publishing India Pvt. Ltd
4th & 5th Floors, Corporate Centre
Plot No. 94, Sector 44, Gurugram – 122003, India

Typeset in Sabon LT Std 11/15.6
by Manmohan Kumar, Delhi

Printed and bound in India
by Manipal Technologies Limited, Manipal

FSC
www.fsc.org
MIX
Paper from responsible sources
FSC® C043100

For our children

Today is where your book begins
The rest is still unwritten
– Natasha Bedingfield, 'Unwritten'

You don't know who I am. But you'll have to trust me on this. Because I'm going to tell you something now. It's about four people you might know. One may even be you. Or me. There are some secrets that have to stay secret.

There's enough going on in our lives in the years after we hit twelve, without fate backstabbing us too...like the oil spots we can't scrub away from our foreheads, the hormones we can't control, the swagger of cool we can't let slide, the doubts we can't scour off our minds. We're trying to be the best versions of who we can be, we really are. Adults don't get that. Almost never. It's just so tough! We feel like we're slipping, our fingers worn out from the nail-biting pressure or the phone-tapping obsession, those fingers are too tired to hold on.

Back to the story, though. So easy to stray off topic. All that research on our nano attention spans. But we like games, right? Puzzles. Riddles. So here's one.

Get this. Four people, high-schoolers, say, you, me, (though we'll use aliases for now) who don't really hang out together – hey, who don't even like each other all that much. But there's this one party where everyone collides. And the fireball starts rolling – and that's just the beginning.

Nothing's ever going to be the same after this. No backspace.

The party's going to see a heart breaking. You can even hear the 'crack' right across the room, over the thumping music. In another corner, a mask will slip and reveal raw fear. Someone will be driven to the point of no return. Another is headed for a crash. Who will escape and who won't, and who will pay for it?

So, you want to know who's who and how they got so tangled with each other. And you want to know who I am and where you fit in. Sorry, you weren't listening. I said right in the beginning...there are some secrets that have to stay secret.

As for those that spill out: they lie there, ticking, ready to explode in your face, daring you to deal with them.

Life's like that.

1

ALISHA

Look at me spinning. See my beads, bracelets, bands clattering as I swirl around. Orbits. Whizzing lights around me. Had too much to drink at this party, I know. Shouldn't even drink, I know. Stop with the warnings. I want to – who's to stop me? What if I want too much? If I want to live in a series of too-muches. Look at Alisha, they should all say, she's Too Much! The life of this party. Except that I feel like I'm spinning too fast. Over the terrace. Over the edge. I'll be leaving this party. On my own terms.

AK

Why's she acting like that? Like she's flipping crazy, dancing in those dizzying circles. Scarf, chains, skulls, beads flying. One pendant almost gouged out my eye. But I'm not cribbing. I'm here for her…her rock. No one messes with me, all right? Doesn't she see that? Don't they all see that? It's time they did. This party's going to be the place they will all learn who rules. Total domination. Now or never. So be warned. Minions! (Just thought I'd add that.)

RUHI

Should I leave everything behind and make this leap? Leave sweet little, good little, Ruhi behind in her pink-clouded bedroom and make it to the party? I can't. What if they find out? What if my folks find out I'm not as good as they think I am? What if my friends find out I'm just too good to be true? What if I find out who I really am, and don't like me? It's just a party, no big deal and no big leap, there's no harm in my going. None at all. Is there?

SHARAD

There isn't an exam I can't crack. But I'm illiterate – when it comes to people. I can't read them, even though I've got the thickest specs in class, ha ha. So it's pointless being here-comes-Sharad-the prize-winner when I feel they're really saying, 'Oye, loser!' Well, it's all going to change today. Tonight. At this party. Where my goddess will swish her wand and voilà – she'll make me as cool as she is. I'm religious that way, ha ha. I worship Alisha. Just wait and watch, folks, this party is where it's All (with a capital A) going to change. Watch!

2

SHARAD

You never know what's behind a closed door.

Nirvana, or the netherworld?

But then, it's not every day that I'm invited by a goddess. To the top of the world – the twenty-ninth floor, people! So I'm hoping it's the former – the happily-ever-after-place, you know.

Nine minutes later, after nine jabs at the doorbell and subjecting this huge, triple-locked door to my infamous metal-melting stare, it's still shut. By rights it should silently swing open on its polished brass hinges to allow me entry into this penthouse party where, as it happens, the happening crowd of my class is. Right now.

Except, I'm not one of them. Should I stay or should I go?

Got it, I'll toss a coin. Entire cricket matches are decided on that. Oh – no coin. I'll toss the anti-anxiety pill my mom's been prescribed instead. Heads, I head into the party. Tails, I turn tail and go home. Wait, what's heads on a pill? Too late – tossed – swallowed.

The legend on the door reads 'Mrs and Mr Arora'. Who are in Turkey. (May they have fun there!) Which is why Aman Arora is throwing this party. Let me get back to focusing on this door. Laser-beam stare. *The sun's rays do not burn until brought to a focus* – Alexander Graham Bell says from among those dozens of quotes I've pasted over my walls at home.

Bell works! Doorbell or A.G. Bell – one of them has done the trick. The door is opened by a girl I don't know. She pushes past me and storms off. Oh, well, it worked, kind of.

I walk through the portal. And – I am IN! And instantly lost. I melt into the wall, squint in the dark at blurred shapes bobbing around in the flashing lights to the throbbing music, until they morph into familiar entities. Murali, Jonathan, Mihika. I move slowly to the periphery of a cluster of my classmates who are laughing. I couldn't catch the joke. I laugh uproariously. It feels great to be in, one of the in-gang. It would be awesome to hang out with these fun guys. But I've got to go find my goddess, remember? Focus! It's what got me a lifetime of A's.

To make it clear, I'm not some sleazy stalker. I'm not teetering on the edge of reality. See, she pinged me last week, Alisha. Some question about the endocrine system. I explained it and we ended up chatting for an hour. I couldn't sleep the rest of the night. I mean this is Alisha we're talking about. Alisha! She said she'd see me at the party. And when someone who's cool orders…tells, not orders…someone who's not… Get my drift?

Who decides who's happening? Ever wondered?[1]

But now there's no Alisha here and my eyes are bouncing about quicker than the strobe. I stop a girl with a tray of tall glasses with what I'm guessing are cokes.

'I'm so hot,' I tell her gratefully, downing one of the drinks. She rolls her eyes.

The second whatabrilliantcoke burns its way down like a chem experiment. Not that I am in the habit of swallowing chem concoctions. I don't even binge-drink cough syrup. Feeling funny now. I need some more coke. Come back, curl with the gokes! She's going up the stairs. Maybe Alisha is upstairs. Up I go then. Feeling light. Feeling trippy.

I trip over the first step.

The girlsthecokeswith says, 'Watch it. You okay?' She helps me up.

I make it upstairs and begin to cough. It's oxygen-deficient here. Bodies crammed together, dancing. Hazy lights. Smoke.

If I squint, I can see shapes silhouetted against the light filtering in from the terrace. And – there – in a stop-frame, stop-time, stop-heart moment – I see her.

Alisha. I'd know the beautiful shape of her beautiful head any beautiful where, even without this beautiful coke.

She's so beautiful I can't breathe.[2]

She's dancing with AK. He's like the Hulk. Tall. Pumped. Green. Okay, not green. I'm green. Ha ha.

1. *Ever felt like this? You're not alone. Want to know what a psychologist thinks about it? Go to 'Talk Space' on page 189.*

I wave. 'Hey, Alisha!' The music and the dark swallow it up. I push my way through to her. 'Hey, Alisha, I'm here.'

She turns and looks at me. Straight in the eye. I give her my best cokeandnowsmoke totally irresistible smile.

She turns away. I'm in the middle of the crowd, staring at the back of that exquisite head. She continues to sway slowly, her arm thrown around AK.

I get it then. What I will never get, never be. My glass of whatwasoncecoke slips to the floor. The notcoke that's already gone down me is coming back up the same way.

I push past the bodies and make it to the terrace where I bring out the whydidIeverthinkitwascoke into the nearest potted plant.

The party stops. The dancing stops. The world rotating on its axis stops. Everyone's staring at me.

I look at Alisha, silently pleading – tell them now, make it make sense.

She tells AK. 'See, I told you he's delusional. But harmless. Come, dance.'

Someone with kind eyes gives me a tissue. It's the girl with the cokes.

I don't look at her. At anyone. It isn't just the glass that shattered.

3

ALISHA

Look, I'm spinning. Like a crazy blur. Like fan blades gone wild. Like the dervish we saw at the only ever foreign family holiday we've taken. Dubai. 4D3N – 30% off if you pay now! My mother took parathas because 'home food is healthiest'. And my sis fell ill despite all that. 2D2N out of the prepaid package tour, we stayed in the hotel room. Couldn't even see a proper sheikh in a dishdasha. I plastered my nose against those massive glitzy shop windows to look at the glossy bags, shoes, and people inside. My father said, Come on, all that's useless.

Can you blame me now for zoning out? For whirling the thoughts right out of my head. What did Geography Ma'am say? The world rotates at one thousand miles an hour. I should, by the laws of last-term's Physics, be flung right off it. I'm ready – arms stretched out like wings. To be slung out to a distant planet, to meet an alien – a rich, crazy–exciting alien.

'Hey Al, hey!' AK's voice. He holds my elbow. To steady me or to stop me?

'I'm cool,' I say. I *am* cool. I'm the coolest kid I know. The coolest kid you all know – don't forget that!

Don't stop me. I need air. The terrace! I walk out. Leaving AK standing there, scowling.

All these girls clustering around me, trying to look like me. My black lipstick and black nails, black spiked hair, the kajal drawn thick around my eyes so my face looks even paler, veins blue, collarbones sticking out like knives. Yeah, you can't be like me. I'm the only me around.

What's funny is that I come from boring. My family's so dull, I want to yell at them. So content with their midsize car, midsize apartment, midsize minds. Neighbours and relatives dropping in for chatty let's-do-potluck lunches... all of them looking and speaking alike, like bots. Ugly spots, clots, bots! So – so – plain. I'm not one of them. I'm NOT. Why do I want to cry? To stand out here on the terrace of this pricey building that my family could never even dream of living in, and to scream at the stars.

Watch me – I'm different. I don't want their dreary straight-line lives, their small-time satisfaction, their large, happy, idiotic extended family gatherings. Look at who I really am. A brilliant diamond trapped underground, can't you see that? Shine on me, I implore the stars, I'm one of you, not one of them.

Ordinary is the worst thing I can be.[3]

Getting here didn't come easy. They call it manipulation. Like that's a bad thing!? It's good, it's great, it takes masterful intelligence to twist someone around my serpent-ringed little finger. To sit with a cold eye. Watching the rest of the girls gorge on chocolate cake. Till they notice me sipping on diet soda, thin and gorgeous, and then their cake sticks in their throats. They push away their plates. Their envious eyes follow me with AK, the guy with the car, the games, the big house, the rich dad. Do I really want to be with him? Or *be* him?

His dad was in the papers one day, inaugurating one of the towers he'd built, star-kissing and sparkly like this one. I pointed him out to my father. Look, AK's dad is in the news. Impress my father, challenge him, shake him out of his bifocals. He nodded over his paratha – Nice, nice, *beta*! – and turned the page.

I was born to be shimmering, sizzling, not plain. It's ripping me apart and no one can see it. I can't take the 'plain'. And I can't take the pain.

If I can't stop hurting, let me hurt someone else.[4]

I bend over the railing and twenty-nine floors down, on the driveway, I see Sharad go stumbling out. I humiliated him in front of everyone. Why doesn't everyone hate me? I'd hate me if I wasn't me. He looks drunk. He probably is. He has possibly never drunk before. And I've made him do that today. I have the power to change people. To crush people. But why would I do that to someone who's crazy about me?

Because I can.

4

AK

What goes down must come up…and into a flowerpot. That was fun, admit it. Sharad's solo show. Or duet – with that plant.

Loser! Class topper and all that, for what? He can't even hold a drink – literally – ha, dropped the glass. My dad should see him, the way he goes on about Achiever Kids. No, scratch that, my dad should see *me* now. Anyway, back to the partaaay!

This party sucks!

Thinking of my dad has ruined it.

Nah, Sharad's ruined it. Alisha and I had something going on before that.

Honestly, it's Alisha. She's ruined it. She's moved off on to the terrace, left me here, slow-dancing with my glass. Everyone saw her, right? Walking out on me. No one walks out on me! I mean, show some respect, yeah?

No one treats my dad like this.

It's stifling here. My head's on fire. I walk over to the terrace, to Alisha bending over the wrought-iron railing.

She looks so frail, like she'll break. I won't let her break. I've got her. I hold her elbow. 'Hey, Al,' I say softly.

She keeps looking down. I bend over too, and see a staggering figure far below – Sharad? Seriously? She's still looking at him. The Amazing A-Plus Puking Party Pooper? C'mon!

A little more firm now. 'Al, hey! Let's go back and dance.'

'You go. I want to stay here. I want air.'

'Cool, let's go get some air,' I tug at her elbow. 'Let's go for a drive. Come on. I'm fed up with this party anyway.'

She stays where she is. Frail. Strong.

Strong. Stubborn. Stupid. She's making me mad now. Being a tease.

'You wanna come with me? 'Cos I'm leaving anyway. Now!'

A flick of her hair. 'You're going to drive like that? You're drunk!'

Is she really worried? Or merely mocking me? I can't tell – my head's burning up. This party was rockin', but now it's...phew!

Why do I reach boiling point in a microsecond?[5]

I need to break something. I throw my glass at the flowerpot. And stomp out.

Air, yeah, I need air too. Air's a great idea. Leave these losers behind.

I crash my way through the house to the elevator. Down. Down. Down. I'm on my way down. There's that movie where they go right down into the underbelly of the earth. And fight their way back up. Why? I'd stay there – it seemed better than this place for sure.

I'm in the car now. My parents' Audi, engine revving. I'm looking out at the driveway, but all I see is my living room, earlier this evening, my dad behaving like an alpha ape with a bunch of bananas. With four cars, he wouldn't miss one if it danced out in front of him, but because I was asking for his car, it had to be a no.

My mom, who was back from some society fundraiser, threw her bag on the sofa. 'It's only a car. You'll buy another with your small change.' You'd think she was helping me out. But she was just using me as the point of her dagger. They're always in the middle of an ongoing battle. And I make the perfect weapon. Double-edged, to cut both ways.

Dad shrugged. 'He's got to learn to take a no. He's too soft. You've spoilt him. Painting the town red in fancy wheels.'

'Like his father…' She darted a quick look at me, then bit her lip. She opened her bag and threw me a key ring. 'Take my Audi.'

'Your Audi?' my dad laughed. Chilling.

He'd bought her the Audi as a birthday gift last year, at the peak of the Ninety-third Battle of the Bloodthirsty Kashyap Klan. I don't have a clue why. They posted a pic with their arms around each other and the Audi. Our latest baby, the pic said.

'Thanks, Mom,' I said softly, hoping to steer things back to normal.

What's normal? Is a family that clashes like this on a daily basis normal? Or is it just mine?[6]

'I'll take good care of the car, Dad.' I said. 'Really.' He didn't even look at me.

The front door swung open and Neo sashayed in. Like she owned the place. She does. Heir unquestioned. My older sis, back on vacation from her undergrad in the US where, according to her, she's burning the midnight oil, getting a degree in business. According to me, though, she's burning up his money as fast as he makes it. 'Heylo, people,' she drawled and without breaking stride, started yapping about her boyfriend. Who, of course, is brilliant and – let me make this short – all the things Dad expects me to be. 'You'll never guess what Max said today!'

I didn't look at her, of course, because I was looking at my dad. I knew what would happen next. It's been a long-running script. His brow cleared, eyes brightened, and he turned towards her. 'Niharika! What?' His face was so eager, I turned away. And slipped out of the front door.

Rewind over. So back here. Me in the hard-won car. It's been revving up a storm. I'm giving Alisha time to walk down. It's different between Alisha and me, unlike between my folks. We'll be there for each other, forever. She'll walk down any minute now. I know she will.

The elevator stops at the ground floor. The doors slide open. A man trundling a suitcase walks out. The doors close.

I inch the Audi forward, till I can crane my neck to look up at the penthouse. There she is, still bending over the balcony.

Like I care. I don't. I'll show her I don't.

I spin the car out on to the driveway and the Audi responds beautifully, streaking out towards the gate. The security guard leaps out of the way. That's good, yeah! Show some respect.

World, show me some respect!

Alisha, did you see that?

5

RUHI

One flick of the switch and my room's all black. Black as velvet. Black as the little black velvet skirt. The one I haven't worn because it's pink-nightie time now; time for good girls to go to bed.

Look at how good Ruhi is, I can see it in my teacher's eyes when I'm the first to hand in my paper. Look at how good Ruhi is, every mom is itching to tell her kid. I like romantic films. That's all right. No one minds.

I like short black velvet skirts. That's *not* all right.

I like Alisha. I want to be Alisha. That's *not* all right. Alisha, say my parents, no, no, Baby, you're so much better than that. She's...well, so...poor thing!

No way Alisha is a poor thing. Ha! She's partying right now. While I'm in my pink bedroom in bed, under my frilly, floral quilt.

Except that I'm not.

Pillows lie plumped up under my quilt. Sleep well, pillows, be good, Monday's the Bio test.

I wriggle into the black velvet skirt. I wish my knees weren't so chubby. They look like puffed-out cheeks. I pout at the bathroom mirror. Don't I look good? Why does good have to be bad? Bad girls look good in short skirts. That's *not* all right. These voices out of my head – I want them to leave, exit, vanish! I'm going out to have fun, and fun's just fine. Fun's good.

Is everything either good or bad, black or white, true or false? Yes? Or no?[7]

Of course, Mumma doesn't know. But that's only to protect her. What she doesn't know won't hurt her. I'm lucky I've got such a wonderful mother… I love my mother. I just don't want to *be* her. I'm sorry, Mumma. I didn't mean that. Good girls don't think like that.

I line my lashes with the blue mascara I'd picked up from Arien Plaza. It's been waiting for today, stashed away in the bookshelf, along with the skirt. Ten minutes later, I look up again at the mirror. I look at myself and see Mumma instead. I've got to stop this. Off goes the bathroom light! Off!

Footsteps. Outside my door. Papa asking, 'Are you okay, Baby?'

'Mffffff,' I mumble. 'Sleeping.'

'Good. Sleep well. Wake up early tomorrow and study.'

My eyes begin to water. It's the mascara. They love me so much. They trust me so much. I'd rather die than disobey them – disappoint them, I mean. Stupid mascara!

I'm guilty even before I do anything wrong.[8]

Into my balcony. A one-storey jump to the sandpit below. Or a one-step back to my warm, pink bedroom.

Should I risk it?

Do good girls take risks? Do good girls who look good in black skirts take risks?

I jump.

6

SHARAD

Out on the street and bending over again, retching. No one should see me like this. I feel sick, stupid. And that's a laugh because I'm the smartest kid in class, I'm anything but stupid. It's a laugh, but I'm not laughing. Alisha is laughing. Or was.

A broken brick in the pavement. I go sprawling on to the street. Scrambling up, keeling over, walking sideways, swaying.

I can't go home like this. I'd get eaten alive by my cousins. They're vegetarian, but you know what I mean. Macho, mean guys. But they're looking after Maa and me, so I've got to say Thank You. And Sorry. I've got to say Sorry a lot. Get my face pushed into the rice on my plate when the grown-ups are away, look up and say, Sorry, I should have eaten that faster. Get tripped by a jean-clad leg that suddenly popped out of nowhere, and say, Sorry, I should have been more careful.

How about, Sorry I'm so smart while you're all blobs of dough? None of you even came near an A, so just manage the family business while I go on and get that brilliant college degree and the fat starting package and take my mom and me far away and Goodbye and Thank you for your six-bedroom bungalow with statues of white women in Greek tunics carrying vases in a Bangalore garden. Jab in my ribs. Sharad, stop looking at those statues, even those babes are way out of your league. Kushal cackling. Blob #1, by way of introduction.

Why are you always so angry? Maa keeps asking. You've got so much to be grateful for, we're lucky. See how well my brothers take care of us. After your father, you know... How many families would look after their sister and her child like this? And your cousins love you, they're just treating you like a kid brother. We're all one family. They'll all be so proud when you graduate top of your school, top of your state. Just wait and see. So proud of their smart little kid brother.

I switch off halfway. She's delusional. Totally stark raving loony. But she's my mother. And I'm going to lift her out of this one-loving-family farce we're in. That's why it's critical I study till I know the books backwards, go on – test me. I'll tell you what the first subhead is on any page number of any book you pick up… And I study like this so that I can slide smoothly into one of those top engineering colleges and a six-figure monthly salary. And then Alisha will say, I always knew you were a rock star. My mother, I mean, not Alisha.

Hey! Bright lights whizzing closer. Too bright – dim them, idiot! My eyes are doing their own number.

Haven't you heard of dimmers? I throw up an arm to shield my eyes. And then I realize the lights are the least of my problems. The car's coming straight at me.

ALISHA

Sharad staggering away, AK driving away. I made them do that… Me. I'm a goddess. Strong. Powerful. Destructive. Impressive. Empty?

I shoulder my long-strapped sling bag, the one with the grinning skull painted on. Weave through the heaving bodies to the table with the food. No one's touched it yet. Everyone's busy screaming the totally wrong lyrics to the current song and flailing their limbs around. Eww! Like they're laundry twitching on a clothesline. Some dignity, guys!

Quick look around. No one's seen me. Slide the French fries off the plate into my bag. Steal a side glance at the slices of chocolate cake. No, that's too much. Mini samosas, perfect! Into the bag. Oh, all right then, what does it matter anyway? The chocolate cake goes in too. The bag's bulging. Stop!

That door at the end of the corridor, that's been shut all along. I know it's Aman's folks' room. No one's in there. Turn the knob. It opens smoothly and I slip in, unnoticed. Wispy as hookah smoke, slinky as a ghost. Lock the door, and the clock's ticking. Push open the bathroom door – it's all marble and mirrors. That's how the penthousers live. That's how I should live. I sit on the marble slab holding the washbasin, and with a sudden urgency clawing at me, I begin to eat.

Down, down, don't waste time biting or chewing, Alisha. I choke on the tip of a samosa but just swallow, my eyes watering. This is beautiful. I am crying as I eat, eat, eat. Till the bag is empty. Tears of joy. The food's lovely. Warm. Kind. Caring. It makes me feel more loved than anyone ever has before. The food loves me whether I'm perfect or not. Who else does?

Will I find perfect love if I don't look perfect?[9]

I allow myself two minutes to stay in this marble-walled paradise, to admire the paintings of waterway-veined Venice on the walls. Why Venice? All that water for a bathroom? And then I feel the heaving from within. Time up! Paradise is shut for the day.

I bend carefully over the toilet bowl, kicking the white rug away with my shoe. And then I stick my finger deep into the back of my throat.

When it's all over, I look at Venice again. Straighten one of the pictures, stroke the boat in the canal going somewhere, lucky boat. I'm crying. Not tears of joy, this time. No.

RUHI

The party is loud. This is what I've been missing all along. This is crazy. Tonight, I am crazy happy fun weird bad. Tomorrow, I will be good.

There's Sani, Rohan, Murali, Jonathan, Aman, Trisha. Having fun. 'Hey Mihika, what's that? Coke? Thanks. Who are the others I don't know? Those older guys don't look like eleventh graders. College?

Cute too.' Giggle. Like I'm in the middle of Mumma's TV serial.

'Where's Alisha?' I ask Mihika.

'Whaaa? Can't hear.'

'Helloooo! Where's Alisha?' I'm shouting.

'Where's what? The loo?'

That sets off uncontrollable giggles. We both clutch each other, laughing hysterically. She sways off, arms up, to melt into the dancing, screaming crowd in the middle of the room.

I hold my arms up too and sway. Look at my little black skirt. I'm about to follow her when I feel a hand on my shoulder. One of those college guys. So yummy-looking. I smile at him, Alia-Bhatt style, I hope. No one's ever asked me to dance before. Tonight's turning out super fun crazy wild bad. Oh, he's not asking me to dance. He's pulling me out of the crowd.

'You're looking for Alisha?'

I must have done something – nodded or something – because I couldn't say much over the noise and, of course, because I couldn't stop smiling. I could barely tear my eyes away from his silver eyes. Have you seen *Twilight*? He's holding out a glass. Good girls don't accept strange drinks. From strange guys. With strange silver, hypnotic, brilliant eyes. But why not?

Only for tonight? No, no. 'No thanks,' I manage finally. Drinks are drugged, remember? Party drinks with date-rape drugs. And I don't know – though I wouldn't mind knowing – him. Why do I keep giggling?

He lowers his head to my ear. 'Alisha's left. Want to go find her?'

Good girls don't go trotting after silver-eyed guys from *Twilight*. What if he turns out to be a vampire? Giggle.

I run the back of my hand over my upper lip. It's hot and smoky and airless here.

'Have a sip. It's safe. Trust me, you'll like it.' He's asking me to trust him, and what if I don't? What kind of a person would I be? Baby, don't trust strangers, says Mumma in my other ear. That's why we have two ears, see? But I'm not a baby. I take a gulp. Nice! It tastes like a coke. Trust him. The world is full of nice people, look at the rainbows, not the drink. Not the rain, not the not the drink. Muddled!

'Finish it off and we'll go find Alisha,' he promises.

Okay then. I knock it back. He laughs. I like his teeth. White. Pointed. Pointed? It's the lights – bright, dazzling, dizzying. He offers his arm and I hold his elbow. Baby and Twilight. This feels so good. He's leading me across the red carpet. Awards Night Red Carpet? Carpet that's whirling around, lights swirling around, I'm rhyming around. Okay, out through the door. Out of the party? But I just got here, look at my little black velvet skirt.

AK

It's supposed to be like a movie, Alisha and me. 4-3-2-1 – at the last moment, she walks out, slow-mo, over to me, as I wait in the car. But she didn't. I couldn't make her. I can't do anything. Despite all the bragging, the biceps, I'm a non-starter, a nobody, nowhere near my dad. Just the opposite.

Not true. I control this car. Look at it leap to my slightest command. My foot gently presses the accelerator. And it's zipping. Everything outside is a blur. Deserted streets. Street lights, shop lights – all slashes of gold. Just one hand on the wheel, just one finger even – a casual swipe, and the car whizzes from one side of the street to the other. The sheer power of this metal monster. All at my command. Dizzying!

I'm on top of the world. No one can touch me here, not my warring parents, not my overachieving sis, not backstabbing Alisha or that bunch of losers. I'm speeding into another realm.

Faster. Faster. Look at the needle move.

You tell me not to take risks. Don't you trust me?[10]

What's that? On the street, weaving about. Get off the street. Get out, idiot! No!

There's no time to react. Mid-breath, I spin the wheel and slam on the brakes, but I'm going too fast. There's a scream of rubber tearing on the road. Or am I screaming? Or that person I've hit? Omigod, I've hit someone.

And then everything goes bee-stung crazy. The car's spinning around, tyres shrieking, lights burning – and then a smash that plunges everything into darkness and quiet.

7

SHARAD

I hold my arms up at the lights speeding towards me...they draw closer and closer still. I dive on to the pavement. The car's almost upon me now, climbing the kerb. What's he doing? What am I doing? I'm going to be sliced into two. A statistic in tomorrow's paper.

What a fine student Sharad was, the principal will say at my memorial service. Alisha will turn her beautiful mascara-streaked face to the camera. The girl with the cokes will be there too, in her little black dress. But we just met, she will say, and cry. My classmates, wearing black armbands, will hug each other and hold up black roses and black placards. Who would help them with their calculus? My weeping cousins will fling themselves at the pyre in remorse, saying, We love you, we should never have pushed your face into the rice. And then orange flames will leap out of the blackened logs. And they will all turn and leave, and go on with their lives.

Except Maa.

RUHI

Silver teeth, pointed eyes. That can't be right. In a party that's whizzing by. That can't be right either.

I'm not in the party. I'm in a car.

Loud laughing. Guys in the car laughing. What's the joke, tell me, tell me. I'm having fun tonight.

I can see the backs of two heads, one with a headband – he's driving. I'm in the back, with an arm around me. Twilight's. He's laughing too.

Brilliant. Lucky. Fun. Funny. Scared. Sick. Not funny. Not lucky. Brave.

'Who are you?' I say.

Twilight turns, startled. 'Hey, she's awake. Hi, baby, are you feeling okay now?'

I'm not a baby, only Mumma and Papa call me Baby, my name is Ruhi – I say this in my head. My tongue feels too thick to make words. He's moving his head in closer.

Is this how it happens? Love? Who is he? But the sneaking question that hits me is – Who am I? Why is this silver-eyed stranger kissing me? Am I supposed to melt, weak-kneed? He's cute. I'm flattered, but is this it? Is this that thing about which songs are written, is this love?

How does forever love start?[11]

I pull my head back.

'Hey, you didn't seem to mind earlier,' he laughs. Joking. Teasing. Cute.

Whaaa? Wait! This happened earlier? When? What earlier? What's now? Where am I? Who is he? Who are they? What happened with whom and when? With a rising panic, I feel like it's a Reference to Context question in my exam. And it will be the first time I don't know an answer.

'Are you taking me home?' I say. Brave.

'No, you're having fun, aren't you?'

'My parents will be waiting for me. They've put a GPS locator on my phone.' Brave. Smart.

'Tell them you're having fun.'

No, I'm not. No fun. No. Frightened. Fighting.

A no is a no is a no is a no is a no.[12]

I whip around and reach for the door handle.

I have a millisecond before they all realize what's happening. I will get away. Or is it too late? Or was it already too late when whatever happened earlier, happened? No, there's no such thing as too late. Twilight's arm is still loosely draped around me, but I use every bit of strength that's in my petite five foot two inches to throw myself against that door. I'm praying Let it be open. Please, God. Please. I'll go back to being perfect. Please, God. The door. The handle. His arm. My arm.

SHARAD

I'm supposed to be giving Maa a better life, not taking it away. And I am her life. She's told me that a gazillion times. Her life. Her pride and joy. Moron with the blazing lights and the zipping car, you can't do that to my mother. I'll kill you if you do.

But I'll be dead.

No, I won't. I can't let myself just give up and exit scene here. I leap to the left. And when it's almost upon me, the car swerves and spins out of control. It smashes into the trunk of a jacaranda tree. And a shower of lilac rains down on it.

He didn't kill me.

I killed him.

RUHI

My hand's on the handle of the car door, pressing the unlock button. A click.

'Hey, wait, I'm not going to hurt you,' he's saying and they're saying, 'Don't let her jump out,' and the guy who's in front who is not the driver is saying, 'Hit the central lock, bro,' and the guy who's in front who is the driver is saying, 'It's friggin' broken.'

And I know that I've been thrown a lifeline.

I throw my weight against the door again and it flies open; I tumble out. My shoulder hits with a force I'll calculate later in class, and get right. Please let me get back to class.

The car's screeching to a stop.

Twilight is leaning out from the back seat and shining a light into my eyes. It's his phone. He's showing me a pic of two people together. And he's shouting, 'Don't do anything silly. Remember I have this.'

And I'm rolling, rolling, rolling – in the gravel by the side of the road. And it's all going black again. And I fight to stay conscious, to stay with the light. If I don't, they will get me back into the car. I will myself to keep rolling, my shoulder feels like it's tearing off. And then I lose the light.

It goes black.

8

ALISHA

Back to the party. Swaying, sashaying, showing them how. Dancing like, what's that they say about no one looking? Except I know everyone is, in awe. Eyes closed, trancing. Beads, anklets, chains, bracelets twirling. Gaming it!

Everything is a scam. Except the secret.

The secret's safe.

The crowd's thinning now. Time to make an exit. Can't be among the last to leave. That's lame.

Eye the crowd for my worker bee for tonight. Now that AK's gone off in a huff of smoke and exhaust fumes.

Javed has his brother's bike, right? Lock eyes with him. Let's leave the boring details out. All I need is to smile and say – 'Can I get a ride home?' No one says no. To a goddess.

We're thundering through the streets – silent, lonely, mist-draped streets. Javed's helmet is perfect. Because he doesn't talk, and I don't. A hand lightly on his jacket-clad shoulder. Feeling one with the bike as it flattens on sharp bends. The wind whipping my hair about my face, stealing my stole.

'Drop me here,' I shout into the side of his helmet. It's nowhere. Just on the street outside a scatter of shops.

Javed screeches to a stop, pulls up his visor. 'Here? Where's your place?'

'I want to walk,' I say, 'thanks.' Swing my leg off. Smile. Turn my back. Walk away. Know he's still looking at me. I sway a little more.

I don't really want to walk. I just don't want him to see where I live. How pathetic the block of apartments is. Pinkish, oldish, paint peeling, verandas grilled, clothes strung out of windows. The block of rock that houses the diamond.

I'm ashamed of where I come from, and ashamed of being ashamed.[13]

Against the thundering away of the bike, I turn full circle and backtrack to a lane, slink along for a few hundred metres and then turn left again, into an even narrower lane, and finally to the gate. No uniformed security guard here. No CCTV. The plumber who doubles up as everything else is asleep in the small cabin in which he cooks his meals. Scale the gate and drop lightly on the other side. Scan the cars parked without a square inch of space between them, the cycles and bikes squeezed in between. Then gaze up at the building, at the fifth floor where my mother's sari (eww!) hangs over the balcony like Rapunzel's escape to nowhere.

I can't go home. Can't ring the bell at two in the morning. Can't bear to see the disgust in their eyes – 'It's Alisha gone wrong again, proving us right once more.'

Crawl under an old car in the furthest corner, backed up against the boundary wall. Pull the skull bag over me. The goddess huddles into a deflated ball against the cold. Curled into a zero.

SHARAD

I want to run away. Except that I can't. It's like the horror draws me in. The murderer always returns to the scene of crime. Why did that come into my head? Run, run! No one can link me to this. I didn't do anything anyway.

I stagger over to look at the crashed car from a foot away. The hood's smashed up into a squat nose, like after a bad boxing match. Windscreen smashed, glass splintered, smoke rising. One driver, with a cloud over his face. An airbag deflating quickly. I see the driver. And then do a double take. The kind you see in movies.

It's karma.

I mean it's AK. The guy who stole Alisha. The girl who ditched me. For the guy who's here now, wrecked. That's the mixed-up equation. It's justice. This is how it will end. AK will drop out of the race, like in all good movies. And Alisha will come to cry on my shoulder, after I've cleaned the notcoke off this jacket, of course.

It's not a movie.

I can't leave a guy like this. He could die. He should die. He didn't spare me a second thought, did he? We've been classmates for years, and he didn't try and help me while I heaved my insides out into that potted plant. He left me to pull myself out of it. I will leave. I can't leave him. I should. It's what God wants, is what Maa keeps saying. It's fate, it's karma, we're powerless. I'm powerless. No, I'm not. I've got the power right now over life or death. His, not mine.

Does fate decide, or do I?[14]

In all the movies, the smoking car is followed by an explosion. That means I don't have too long to pull him out. What if he's dead already? He's staring at me glassy-eyed. Maybe he has amnesia? Every movie has someone ending up with memory loss, it's as common as the common cold. There are over two hundred strains of the common cold, which makes some of them quite uncommon. There are two hundred thousand movies with amnesia. Stop. Screen heroes don't waste time thinking of the flu virus when they've got seconds to save someone. What if the blast goes off while I'm in there, pulling him out? I'll leave him. It's self-defence. I need to protect myself.

AK

I'm alive.

Or am I dead? It's all a white cloud, so maybe I'm in heaven. Have I gone blind? Then the airbag deflates and I see a face up close and personal. It's Sharad. Surely he's not the one person I meet in heaven? What are the chances! He's staring at me like I'm a lab specimen.

Am I? Is my head smashed in? Maybe I'll have a face replacement and get to be someone else.

Got to get out of this. I turn to unbuckle my seatbelt, and that's when heaven flips over 180 degrees. Hell in multicoloured pain. A bolt of red-hot lead shoots up my wrist through to my shoulder to the base of my skull and ends up in the back of my mouth. I scream. I'm stuck in here, my left arm's trapped and I can't get my right arm out to unlock the seatbelt. My arm looks mangled, like it's inside out, wet, burning, throbbing. Scream.

That idiot Sharad's still staring at me. He's backing away. What's wrong with him? Can't he see I need help? Help me, you duh! Except the words are inside my head. I can't ask him to help me. I can't ask anyone, I'll look weak. And I've never been weak.

I try to twist my body around so that my arm can reach over to press the unlock button, and I scream again. I scream every obscenity I know (and I know a whole lot). But what I'm actually whimpering is, 'Help me!'

Sharad turns and gulps, and it strikes me that he's looking unhinged himself, sort of shaky. He tugs at me. No! I scream again. 'Stop!'

'Get out,' he says. 'There's smoke coming out of your car…it may explode.'

Genius! How did he get to be a class topper? 'If I could get out, I would have. I can't. I'm stuck. My arm's stuck. My seatbelt is stuck.'

He leans across me, over my throbbing arm, and I scream some more. He clicks the seatbelt free. Finally.

He drags me out in a heap on to the grass verge, with me yelling all the time, my right arm flapping like an empty sleeve on a clothesline.

He's way too skinny, I'm probably twice his weight. Somehow, he inches on, managing to drag me, like a sack of bricks, across the grass till he's calculated (hey, he's the math topper!) that it's a safe enough distance from the car. And then – get this – he walks away.

'Hey, Sharad!' I call out. 'I need to go to a hospital.'

'Yeah, you do,' he agrees, nodding at me lying crumpled, sweating, bleeding, blabbering. And he's still stumbling away.

I fumble around with my left hand and manage to extricate my phone from the pocket of my jeans. I curse freely while I'm doing it. The pain is something else. Why can't I just black out?

And then a cold splash of reality... Who am I going to call?

Dad? Mom? Niharika? Ha! Not without telling them I've trashed the Audi. Omigod, I've trashed the Audi. Dad will kill me. I've survived a car crash, only to be throttled later.

Alisha? She's the one I'm closest to. Was close to? I call her. It rings out. Pick up, Al, please. I call again. Twice. Five times. Seven times. She doesn't answer. After all we've been through, she doesn't care.

My arm's bleeding out, and I'm beginning to feel faint. I lie back on the grass and look up at the sky. Is it better out there, after all this is over? I feel the sting of tears just behind my lids. I don't want it to be all over. Not yet. I'm only seventeen. Not so big and macho and tough any more. Just someone who's reached dead end. I've been strong too long. But I can't do it all on my own any more. Someone help me.

'Okay, I'll take you to the hospital, but you better have cash.' Sharad's leaning over me. He has come back. I'm crying openly now, and he's saying, 'It's okay. I've got you.'

ALISHA

Is that a rat? Scuttling around my ankle? Shake my leg, bite down on my fist. It's cold here, and my teeth keep chattering. I'm curled up into a tight foetal position. The old, paved car park has prickly grass growing between the cracks. Hold your breath, Alisha, hope no one, no rat, no human, will find you. You can't be discovered here…

The phone rings and I almost shriek. It's like so sudden. I slap at it, trying to silence it. Has the sleeping plumber heard? It's AK. So full of himself. Calling to ask, I guess, why I didn't join him. How I blah blah left him blah blah…like everything's about him. Mute the phone. It rings again, vibrating, lighting up. I kill the call. Again and again. Then I switch the phone off.

It's a cold clear night. If I stretch out from beneath the car's underbelly, I can see the stars. My beautiful stars. But I won't. Because they shouldn't see me. Not like this. No one should.

9

RUHI

When I open my eyes, usually it's to sunlight slanting across my bedroom ceiling that's plastered with glow-in-the-dark stickers of hearts and balloons. Sometimes I wake up to Mumma-Papa smiling over me, she, fussing over my hair, holding out a mug of morning milk, he, delivering some inspirational line for the day. This time I open my eyes to darkness, to two faces peering at me, but faces I've never seen before.

The rewind is quick: throwing myself out of the car, rolling down the embankment at the side of the road, slamming into something that made it all go black. Curtains. End of Scene.

The car's moved on, I guess, because these are different men. They don't look like they've been to a party. They're on their way back from a night shift, I'm guessing, because they still have their sweat-and-oil-stained maroon uniforms on with something-Sagar-Hotel embroidered on the pockets. They frown.

Men. Strangers. All sorts of switches trip, red lights flash, my head clears swiftly. I swing my arms out at the two men. 'Wait,' one says. 'We saw you fall out of a car.' And the other says, 'Where do you live, we'll take you home.' Don't trust strangers, Mumma says. Trust me, says a stranger with silver eyes.

I roll out from under the overhang of their shadows. Doing a lot of rolling lately – helps to be shaped like a rolling pin, the shape I've hated all my life. I pull myself up to my feet and run. I have never made an athletics team in my life, but now I run like my life depends on it. My life does depend on it.

My tight little skirt is almost impossible to run in. I realize I have one platform-heeled shoe on. I kick it off. I run faster.

'Wait!' I hear them shout after me.

Not likely! I race on, and when I realize there's no sound of footsteps pounding after me, I risk looking back. They're still standing there, the two of them, under the scant light of a street lamp, studying me, perplexed. Not their regular night, this. To find someone unconscious, who suddenly springs up and charges away. They may have been good guys, after all. No. There are no good guys. None. Not after tonight.

They don't follow me. They look at me until I disappear around the corner. Maybe they did just want to help. I run on, my long hair flapping behind me, stomach knotting, breathing hard. I recognize this neighbourhood, it isn't too far from home, a couple of kilometres at most. It's just that I've never been sporty. Chess was the only sport I trained in. Good students don't waste precious man-hours huffing pointlessly around a field or hitting a ball with a bat.

Or going to parties.

Or drinking.

Or pushing off with strangers.

It's that greyish light before dawn when I get home. My run has long since waned into a brisk walk, and then just a shuffle. I find the housekeeping ladder where I know it's kept, propped up against the back of our building. I heave it over to lean it against the balcony of my room and climb up. Once up, I kick the ladder away. I'm home. Safe. At last. Why did I ever leave?

I turn on the shower. The water's cold, and I scrub myself till I'm red and raw. I scour my tongue, teeth, cheeks. The bathroom mirror shows a bruised young girl. In more ways than the mirror could know. The left side of my body is scraped, and my lip has a cut. I pull on my nightdress and manage to make it under the quilt just before I hear Mumma's footsteps. 'Baby, are you having a shower at this hour? I heard the…oh sorry, must have been downstairs.' She leaves and I breathe again. Safe.

Tucked under my quilt, glow-in-the-dark hearts above – nothing can harm me now. Safe.

My phone pings. It's an unknown number. And a message:

Remember I have the pic

ALISHA

The milkman's moped sputters to a stop outside the gate. The pale light tells me it's breaking dawn. A respectable hour. He will ring the bell and my mother will collect the blue-and-white plastic packets, and within that small window of time before my parents go out for their morning walk, I can slip in. They usually leave the door unlocked.

Kick off your shoes, Alisha, tread softly behind the milkman. He stops at every floor. I hear a bell rung sometimes and the splat of a milk packet dropped into a basket at others. I duck into the stairwell just below, each time. He gets to the fifth floor and rings our doorbell with its distinctive trill of 'Old MacDonald Had a Farm'.

'Cold today.'

'Yes, bad weather. One extra litre. Making kheer.' My father's voice.

The exchange is over and the milkman proceeds up the stairs. Noiselessly, I move to the door, shoes in my hand. The door's ajar. No voices. No light. I slip in.

And come face to face with my father.

I stand there in my bare feet, shoes in hand, shivering, black spangled jacket barely covering my shoulders, kajal smudged, lipstick smeared. My father stands in his spotless white kurta-pyjama, looking at me. It's five on a chilly Bangalore morning.

Shout. Rant. Rage. Call me names. Say how terribly I've behaved: I want to say to my father.

Then pull me into a hug – it's cold. Remember, you told the milkman that? Ask me where I was, what went wrong: I don't say any of it, of course.

He stares at me, no reaction at all, then walks into their bedroom. I hear my mother's voice, 'What was that?'

His reply. 'Nothing. No one. Not important. Ready for the walk?'

AK

So now we're in a hospital. Skipping the horror of the cab ride, which is agony to even recall. Every bump in the road, every slight bend, every time the driver braked. Can you hurry? It hurts. Can you slow down? It hurts.

Emergency stretcher. The duty doc shining a torch into my eyes, nurse taking my blood pressure and the questions pelting like rain against a window. Do you have insurance? Where are your parents? Does it hurt? (They've got to be kidding, right?) Do you feel nauseous? Can you sign here? Who is this boy? Lift your leg. Is he related to you? Any pain in your head? Can you stick out your tongue? Is this a police case? How old are you? Are you allergic to any medication? How much did you drink?

The X-ray shows a fracture of the radius near the wrist. The lacerations across my arm from the shattered windscreen caused all that copious bleeding.

My blood group is B+. Can you let me leave? I can't call my parents. I forgot their number. I must have concussion. No, I don't want an MRI. I lost my phone. Whoa, that hurts! My brother will take me home. This is my brother. Yes, he looks different. Sharad, have you got any ID proof? His surname's different. He's taken my stepdad's surname. No, I can't move my shoulder. We have different dads. No, I can't remember my dad's phone number. He can't either. They don't get along. I don't know why. That hurts, stop it. Just patch me up and send me off, okay? I have a credit card. Here. I'm over eighteen.

I can tell no one believes me.

Cleaning up, injections, stitches on my upper arm, forearm in a cast, sling around my shoulder, hooked up to a drip. It will be morning soon. Sharad's nodding off on the chair beside my bed, head bent over his phone. What if he'd not been there? What was he doing there anyway?

The nurse wakes him up to go buy replacements for the drugs they've used. 'Take my wallet,' I say. He takes it. He gets back and sits staring at me morosely. Like I messed up his red-carpet-night plans.

'Look,' I get to the point immediately, 'I can't go home. My dad will roast me. Can I come to your place?'

He begins to laugh. Not at all the reaction I expected. He says, 'My cousins would love you. You're the opposite of me. You're a cool, tough, testosterone-filled egg-puff like them.'

I'm not sure that's a compliment. I squint doubtfully at him and then chuckle too. 'Epic! And my dad would love you. More than he does me. You're this smart achiever type, like him.'

Wish it were that easy. An exchange. 'Has my face been bashed up enough for a transplant? We could exchange faces – and lives.' That gets him laughing some more, and me too, though my ribs seem to be cracking apart. I wonder what it would be like to be in his egg-puff family, though.

It's weird how often other families seem better than your own.[15]

'I don't want your life,' Sharad says. 'The only cool thing you have is that car, and now it's smashed.'

Idiot! Now, I'm back to agonizing over the Audi.

SHARAD

Set out to have the coolest, most awesome party night of my life. And end up babysitting a gorilla in hospital. Anyway, it will make a good excuse back home. Maa will go gooey at my kind-heartedness. She'll probably want to bring AK hot, home-made meals.

How people treat you is their karma; how you react is yours – Wayne Dyer says that from my wall, and Maa says all good deeds pay off. Therefore, any time now Alisha will call me and say she's sorry and she doesn't know what came over her.

So why am I still stuck here? Shouldn't that karma start kicking in? But I'm signing forms, buying meds. I use some of the cash from his wallet to buy myself a sandwich at the hospital canteen. It tastes like crêpe bandage. He slips me his phone before they cut his shirt away, so they can't call his father. I ping his father:

> Your son is in Super Speciality Hospital!
>
> Come immediately!!!

Was sorely tempted to add: Transfer five million into my bank account if you want to know which room. But I'm a nice guy. So I didn't. And then I remembered AK and Alisha, and added:

> Your son will survive. Your car did not

After half an hour of them prodding and scanning him, I can barely keep my eyes open. I've fallen off the chair once already. I begin to swipe through my phone and find this flood of party pics on our class group. How? It was dark, smoky, and no one was clicking that I noticed. Ah, that's because no one was clicking any of me. Oh well, one. Me watering the flowerpot. Nice, you guys. Turds!

Plenty of Alisha, of course. Everyone clicks her. And hey, there's the girl with the cokes.

And the kind eyes.

I see her tagged on it. Tia. A mass of curls framing her round face, the light catching the twinkle in her eyes. Sharad, wake up! You've just got publicly humiliated by one girl, don't go crushing on another.

But still…

Twenty minutes later, I'm still falling off the chair, AK is babbling about something. I ignore him. I pretend to be fiercely attracted to the exciting interface of my phone. And all the pics I'm not in.

And that's when I message her. Who cares? I've lost so much tonight – my dignity, my dream girl and, by the way, my spectacles too (though, in any case, I was seeing double after the notcokes, so that didn't matter too much) – there's nothing left to lose:

Hey, remember me?

Smartest pick-up line in history, I bet.

No reply. Obviously not. Who would remember me?

Where are AK's parents? It's been, like, two hours since I've messaged them. Surely they should have appeared by now, carried him back, dropped me home and given me that five million? And told my thug cousins what a brilliant, brave lifesaver I am?

It's been three hours. First light of dawn. No sign of the Kashyap billionaire parents still. AK babbles on about face swaps. He's funny when he's strung up to the IV drip. Now I'm tired of humouring him. I'm tired of waiting for karma. I'm tired of being the nice guy. I'm tired. Period.

AK

The pain meds have kicked in and I'm feeling spaced out. Sharad's already fallen asleep at an angle so awkward, his neck may touch his hip soon. Has he been swiping some of my painkillers too – why's he so doped?

I'm alone again. No one to talk to, turn to. Not even the loser of the batch (well, prize-winner, but you know what I mean).

And I'm back to thinking about what I should do. About the Audi. About getting out of here. About running away. About staying alive. Then the plot takes a twist…

I hear him before I see him. The loud, demanding voice, 'Why was I not called immediately?' Not 'Where's my son, how's my son?' This is about him.

Who called them anyway? How?

The nurse shushes him angrily. We're in the Emergency Room, eight beds with patients in various stages of pain and drowsiness. Plus Sharad in collapse mode. Silence, she mimes. Or go out.

I can see them through the crack in the flimsy plastic curtain around my bed. In a moment, he's wrenched it aside. And there's no more defence. Just him versus me. Him and me, I mean. That came out wrong.

My mom appears from behind him, dressed like she's going for a brunch at the Club. She's had time to put on the pearl necklace and lipstick, I notice, even as she'd been rushing to see her son in hospital. She squeezes my shoulder. Ow! But if I'm honest, what really hurts is not my mom's touch, but my father standing there, not touching me.

No mention of the crashed car. When will that hit me?

He takes control, of course, and the staff soon bend to his will. Discharge summary, meds list, payment invoices. Send the driver to get this, buy that.

Sharad has woken up with all the ruckus. My mom's looking at him quizzically, since he's occupying the only chair beside my bed, which prompts him to jump up, saying, 'I brought him here.'

My dad nods. 'Good! Thank you, you will be well compensated.'

'No, no, Dad!' Pure horror now. 'He's not someone you can pay off. He's my friend.'

10

AK

Home sweet home! Arm throbbing. No one around to care. Dad's gone out for golf with his buddies, which will run into late lunch and drinks at the Club. Sunday routines can't be broken even for offspring with broken arms. Neo's door hasn't opened even once; I wonder whether she even knows about my crash. Mom's been on the phone for four hours. Home sweet home!

RUHI

He has a picture of the two of us. He's keeping it to blackmail me. He says it's because he loves looking at it. What if he's fallen in love with me? It's possible. It happens in the movies all the time. One glance and ta-da!

We can't be in love if I don't even know his name. I can't ask him now, not after all we've been through. What exactly is it that we've been through? Should I ask? What does the picture show? What did we do? What's your name? Do you love me?

I've finally got my first boyfriend. And my first reaction is I want to tell the girls, See, I'm not a saint. You had me wrong. 'Sweet little Ruhi' was so deceptive. Because I'm smart, I could see it in the way they stop whispering when I join the gang. I mean, sure I'm friends with everyone. The girls like me. I just notice a fleeting smirk now and then. A look that says, What would you know? Or how, when I sit at the canteen bench and unpack my three-tiered lunch box, the conversation would falter, stop, start again, on safer topics.

'I know, right, he's so...' Giggle. Ruhi enters. Start again. 'So what did you get for lunch today?' Hey, I'd want to say, but didn't know how to, you can talk about stuff with me. I'm not going to tell anyone. I'd like to know. Besides, it's not that I'm an angel. I do bad stuff, like...like...

Like what? I've never even looked over the girls' shoulders at Isha's phone. Not once. I don't want to know stuff like that. I'll wait till I meet someone right, fall in love, get married and all that. It's how it's meant to be. Mumma told me.

And now I've met someone right. Right? It's just that I don't know his name.

What do I tell the girls? What do I tell Mumma-Papa?

Ping!

Asleep?

Twilight. I bite my lip, text back:

Hey!

Hey!

Send me the pic

Say please

Please

Meet me and I'll show you

The curtain in my doorway shifts, a slash of light frames a thin silhouette in the doorway. Papa tiptoes in. I stuff the phone under my pillow and shut my eyes. He's bending over me, brushing my hair off my forehead. 'Baby, it's almost six.'

The phone pings and lights up under my pillow.

Sunk!

Quick, need to save myself. I mumble, 'I know. I've set an alarm.'

He says, 'Big girl now. Papa doesn't have to wake you up any more.' I can hear the smile in his voice, a small sigh too.

'Feeling sick – let me sleep some more,' I murmur, eyes still pinched shut.

He puts the back of his fingers against my forehead. 'Fever? Oh, Baby, you overdo it. Study so much. Sleep, it's Sunday. I'll wake you in an hour.'

Ping. Again. Stop messaging. No, don't.

'Turn off that alarm,' he says as he leaves.

And just like that, I swing from being in love to hating myself. What am I doing? I begin to actually feel sick.

AK

Alisha hasn't answered. I should have known. All she wanted was my car. Car's trashed. Mom in her room,

Neo in her room, me in my room. We've got enough rooms in this enormous apartment for anyone else who wants to come and shut themselves up in a room. Home sweet home!

ALISHA

Empty! One interaction with my folks and yesterday's high crashes.

My sis is asleep in the bedroom we share. She's thirteen, but she still curls up like a baby with her stuffed teddy bear. I don't really want her to grow up. It's no fun from up here. She sleeps on, hair flattened against her cheek. Unaware of what's out there, the stars – the devious, plotting, diabolical stars – sucking your dreams out of you. Out of me. Not you, Moni.

The front door clicks shut. They're out on their walk. I have an hour. One empty hour.

Empty.

The fridge has leftovers from last night's dinner. They had *chhole* without me. A bowl left. Half a loaf of bread sits on the dining table, alongside three bananas, a packet of crisps, all covered with a tasselled napkin. I think of the brushed-steel bowl of fruit on Aman's table. Such a touch of class. I lift the napkin.

White sliced bread, crisps, bananas, cold *chhole* – I swallow all of it. I need more. Snip open the extra-milk-packet-for-kheer-it's-so-cold-it's-winter-only-I-can't-hug-my-shivering-daughter and tilt my head back. Pour the milk down until I feel the pushback.

Rush to the bathroom that Moni and I share. No pics of Venice. No marble. A mirror framed in red plastic and a shelf for our shampoos. Pink tiles with years of black grime creased into the grouting. No amount of scrubbing helps, my mom complains to her sister on the phone, even soda doesn't work. Lean an arm against the wall, and it's out. The *chhole* they had without me, bananas, bread, crisps, milk. Wash the place up and step out.

Moni's eyes are open. 'How was the party? Anyone cute? Anything fun?' Sleep-blurred voice.

'No one. Nothing important.' My father's words. The family motto. Nothing important.

AK

I knock on Mom's door. One-two-three. I knock on Neo's door. One-two. I knock on Dad's door. One. I twist the doorknob and enter Dad's bedroom. Wall-to-wall mirrors track my every move. We're on to you; we know what you want; we know what you do here. I see myself in the mirrors, open Dad's suit wardrobe, rifle through the pockets of his coats, then the trousers, transfer the scrunch of notes I find in a pocket into my own pocket and shut the wardrobe. Hey, I tell no one in particular, Dad's got so much money he won't even know this is missing; he never does. He'll probably think he overtipped someone. I mean he throws money at everyone but his son, right? So I've never seen the harm in helping myself – you want something, just go get it. Ha ha! Just that I'm not laughing. You'd think I'd be used to this by now, but I've got to talk myself into it every single time. And I don't even believe my own excuses myself.

The mirrors show four different angles of the young guy with his arm in a sling head for the door. I don't like him, I don't know why he steals, I don't even know him.

SHARAD

The Beemer purrs through the streets and stops at the gate of our bungalow. After dropping the weirdo billionaires home, their chauffeur is now dropping me back. The sun rising over the white pillars, the alabaster statues endlessly pouring water out of their vases are the only audience I'm allowed. Why aren't my cousins here to see this? Me, chauffeur-driven home in this awesome car.

Not one idiot cousin. No uncle, aunt, grandmother. Not even the gardener watering the lawn.

Waste!

Obviously, only when I'm halfway up the curved marble stairs do I hear Kushal's voice. He's emerged from the dining space downstairs. 'Sharad, come here.'

'Why?'

'Because I said so.'

Yeah! Sure. That's the way it always plays. So I go down. And he says, 'Go upstairs right now; your mom's been worried sick about you.'

Sick, that's what he is, sick. Petty power play. Called me down only to send me back up.

Maa is sitting up in her bed, chanting, praying, her eyes closed. You'd think I'd been on a hijacked plane, instead of at a classmate's party.

I stand near her. Softly, 'Maa?'

She opens her eyes, and I say, 'I'm sorry I didn't call, I didn't want to disturb your sleep, but wait till you hear what happened…' (Note: The first thing I say, almost always, is sorry.)

The next hour. She wants to know all the details. I make them up as I go along. How I was the life of the party. How I totally killed it. How the kids thronged around me and copied my dance moves. ('I didn't know you could dance, *beta*, you must show me,' she says.) How they begged me to help them with maths. In the middle of a party, yeah right. She didn't even blink. She just lapped it all up. How the girls sat together and smiled, while Uncle and Aunty (I hope they're enjoying Turkey!) served us hot home-cooked food. ('No smoking, drinking, drugs and all that, no?') No, no, Maa. That's only in your TV serials, not in real life. I wouldn't do anything like that, you know that. How AK insisted on dropping me all the way home and we tried to avoid hitting some drunk guy, and crashed into a tree. How I carried a comatose AK (the big baboon, yeah right!) into the hospital and the doctors said I'd saved his life. If I'd brought him in a minute later… How his parents came and cried on my shoulder. And when I saw in her eyes the picture of me that I'd painted, I began to believe it myself.

Lies aren't lies when they're just protecting a parent from the ugly truth.[16]

AK

I'm slinking back to my room, my fist still in my pocket, clenched around the wad of cash, crossing the cavernous white living room, when Jaggu Kaka limps in through the foyer, unwinding his muffler from around his head. The keeper of secrets, doer of dishes, cleaner of party-littered carpets, wiper of lipstick-marked glasses, remover of shoes from my dad's feet when he stumbles into bed, lighter of lamps in my mom's room, walker of dogs – our three golden spaniels who make the house feel like a home. Jaggu Kaka bends to click free the leashes from the collars of freshly-walked Simone, Sunshine and Silk. They hurl themselves at me, barking happily, hysterically. I collapse with them on to the thick white rug and sink three inches into it. Jaggu Kaka looks at my sling and comes over to sit cross-legged near me. I do what I've done over the years. I lower my head on to his bony shoulder. He puts an arm as light as his threadbare kurta sleeve around me. I allow my eyes to close, with Kaka and the spaniels around me.

Home sweet home.[17]

11

ALISHA

In my cave all of Sunday. Under my quilt. Won't emerge for lunch, though I hear my mom calling out that it's ready. Twice. Thrice. Moni yanks away my quilt, sees my eyes shut tight and goes out to report that I'm still asleep. I hear the clang of the serving spoons and the lilt of lunchtime conversation. Without me. They're better off without me.

I push away those who are closest to me. Why?[18]

They're hatching a plan to visit my aunt this evening – my dad's sister – a half-hour's drive away. The family will gather, laugh, eat, have a 'fun' evening. Fun! Eyes shut, quick – Moni's footsteps. 'Didi, wake up, please. We're all getting worried.'

'Tell her this won't work.' From the dining room. From my father.

'Didi, this won't work.'

'Tell her we know she's awake.'

'Didi, they know you're awake.'

'Tell her she has to eat lunch, please, she's looking so skinny, so sick.' From my mother.

'Didi, you have to eat lunch, you're looking so...' Moni stops, whispers, 'you look gorgeous, don't worry.'

My eyelids prick. Keep them shut. Tight. Tighter.

Moni leaves.

Three hours later, the rustling of clothes in our wall cabinet. My mother pulling out an outfit for Moni to wear. From the rustle, I can tell it's the orange organza kurta. I was bought a matching one in pink. Enough shimmer on it to light up an underground tunnel. I'd much rather be in that tunnel than in a room bursting at the seams with gurgling relatives.

'Alisha, you can't sleep all day.' My mother tries again. I don't know why she still does.

'Alisha!' She taps my shoulder, draws away the quilt, shakes me. 'Alisha!'

I open my eyes, look directly at her, and say, 'I'm not going with you people.' Turn away to the wall and shut my eyes again. But not before I see the hurt deepen in hers.

Half an hour later, the front door clicks shut. They've left. Without me. What I asked them to do. What I wanted them to. What did I think they would do? That they'd stay back?

I head straight to the fridge, biting my lip so hard that I draw blood.

Food never lets me down.

Binge-eat. Binge-purge. Binge-sleep. Am I trying to get something out of the food, or lose myself in it?[19]

RUHI

I've spent the last hour texting Twilight. It's exciting. I'm exciting. Finally. Look at good little Ruhi. He thinks I'm pretty. He loves my long hair. He loves my eyelashes. Three cheers for the blue mascara! He loves my cheeks, my legs, my lips. I think at one point he's just reading from the chapter on anatomy in a biology textbook. I mean, he's left nothing out. But that's sweet. Right? He likes my smile, my frown. He got all that in the couple of hours we were together. In the short time in which I didn't even get his name?

The only question I keep evading is when we should meet. How? How will I get away? And am I really ready for this? Quick, phone under pillow, the curtain's being drawn aside. A concerned parent's face peeps in. I'm being torn into two. Nice girl. Exciting woman. No one can be both. No. But really – can they? Can I?

SHARAD

If it weren't so miserable, I'd find it funny. Spending hours dabbing on my cousin's perfume for an evening with Alisha in a dimly lit party, only to waste it all on an overgrown ape in the sterile glare of tube lights in a hospital.

Nothing's ever going to go well for me. I'm one of those born losers. I'm never going to find love or luck or happiness or… Who's messaging now? Seriously! Does AK want me to go feed him porridge? Or is it some other idiot with a funny comment on my amazing party performance?

It's from Tia.

The girl with the curls and kind eyes – whoopee! Her message:

Lmk when we cn meet

What? Am I seeing double? Are my eyes deceiving me? The evil AK? Someone's playing a trick on me. Hah. I won't fall for it. My cousins! They're messing with me. Or Alisha being sarcastic?

Who is this?

I message back. Just the right touch of haughty and disbelieving. And add:

I'm busy

She replies:

You msgd me, no?

I take so long to process all the optional replies in my head that she pings again.

Okay. Quick. Lmk when 2 meet

That's amazing. I mean, I didn't even have to ask. Her message:

Look, I cant chat wit myself. R U there? Did U drop dead??

No. No. I'm alive!

Wow! Well done, Sharad… I'm so plumbing the depths in clever comebacks, right?

Gr8. U wan 2 meet me?

I take so long to find something awesome to say that she pings again:

> Look, I have ur specs, dude! U dropped them at d party. By d time I pikd them up U wr outta thr. Wan? Don't wan? M running outta time.

Ah! My spectacles. We should meet so she can return them. Not for my scintillating personality. Not yet.

> Yes. Yes, Returner of Lost Property. Let's please meet.

I send a smiley. She sends a smiley back. That was smart. Finally. I'm brilliant. Fantastic. Happening. We plan to meet at the café near the underground mobile shop on Double Road. On Thursday evening. She does a shift there after class, she says.

Can't stop smiling. Told you there was something in that coke!

ALISHA

I can't stop shivering. My hands are clammy. Burning up from inside. Melting down. It's dark outside and I'm still alone. My phone says it's nine at night. No one's home yet.

The door clicks open finally. Voices. Many. The lights flick on, in the living room, in my room – jarringly.

Curl up tighter, hold the quilt wrapped around me, keep my eyes shut.

Voices. Hands shaking my shoulder. 'Alisha. Get up.'

No. No.

'You've been sleeping like this all day.'

Go away.

Hands pulling the quilt away, lifting me on the bed to a sitting position. 'Listen. Alisha.'

Squint open my eyes. Many faces blurring. Lights are way too bright. Go away. Head throbbing. Talking over each other, clucking, cajoling. Uncles who have taken control, aunts sympathetic, cousins curious, grandaunt worried, parents at the back – helpless. No Moni. At least bring Moni in. Y'all go away.

Alisha, enough is enough. We care about you. You can't go on like this. Get up and get a hold on yourself. Look at you. This has gone on too long. What's wrong with you, Alisha? Look up. Are you on drugs? That's what happens to these youngsters nowadays. Cover her up, she's shivering. *Beta*, we want the best for you. Let us help. You are killing yourself. What's that smell? Is it vomit? Go get her some water. Okay, we are all together now because your parents cannot take care of you alone. Pack your bag now, come with us. Alisha, get up, you want something to eat? Look at your hair, child. Poor girl. What have you done to yourself? Drink some water, here. If it were my child... Alisha, listen now. You've pushed us too far. You leave us no choice.

So many voices. So many faces. Go away. Please.

Okay, you need to come with us now, to Piyush Maama's place. You will be safe. Bad company, that's what it is. Drink water now. Put on a sweater. Take off all those chains. They're strangling you. Come, *beta*, get up now. Pack your bag.

Go away. I hate you all. I don't want to go anywhere.

Sumi, call that doctor you were talking about. That psychiatrist. It is serious now. Alisha, can you hear us? Is she all right? Her eyes are glazed. Omigod. Should we call an ambulance? Okay, drink some milk. How did you let her get to this state? Poor, poor child.

Bile rising. I push them aside and make it in time to the bathroom, slam the door shut. Heave. Let the tears flow too. Hear the voices go on outside. I know what this is called. An intervention. They have come to rescue me, they pity me.

I'm not a 'poor child', you fools! I am a star.

12

RUHI

Sunday's gone in this blur of excitement, guilt, thrill, fear. Hopping out to the dining room to eat with Mumma-Papa and then dashing back to my room, snuggling under my quilt, drawing worried looks from them. At the nth 'Are you sure you're okay, Baby?' I snap. I'm not a baby. I'm a teen. Except I don't say it out loud, of course. Of course!

Give me a time, baby, tell me when

Twilight's texts come in every few minutes. Baby again. Eye-roll. But smile too. It's okay when he calls me 'baby'. He's allowed to. It makes me feel older. Special.

My phone's propped up on page 114 of my textbook – I've been on page 114 all day, by the way. Giggle. I've made sure it's plugged in, charging. In between texting, I look through my group messages. Pics from the party are all over the place.

Dancing, laughing, eating, posing, hugging. Mihika holding up her foot so you can see her new boots. Arush and Hansika doing V for victory poses. Three guys pretending to puke. Sharad actually puking. Ha ha. When did that happen? I missed that. Some 28 comments after that, Aman fooling around with his dad's bar cabinet. Isha dancing on the sofa. Isha falling off the sofa. Ha ha. Oops! 35 comments. Isha exiting the group. Rohan's air-guitar performance. A girl with curly hair, whom I don't know, holding a tray and making a funny face at the camera. The same girl waving. The same girl on the stairs... 'Who's that?' That's from the guys. 'She's from the caterers', 'She's cute!!' 'Shut up', says someone. Hey – what's this – AK grabbing Alisha's arm – 'Uh-oh. Trouble in Paradise,' someone writes. I want to tell them to shut up, but of course, I won't. Leave Alisha alone, I want to say, she's a goddess, she's way above you and your smutty comments. But I won't. No one will bother about what I say. I'm not sure anyone even realized I was there. I can't find myself in a single pic.

I scan the images feverishly. Not in one. There's the girl with the curly hair and the tray in a dozen pics. There's – oh – there's the three guys, including Twilight. 'Who are they?' comments and Aman's replies, 'No idea, guys.' I feel cold. Mumma calls out, Baby, something or the other that ends with a question. I say nothing. I'm invisible, see? Not there in one pic.

Twilight's text lights up my phone:

Hey, disappeared?

He notices me. I'm not invisible to him. He values me. I'm somebody special to him. I'm not feeling that big love yet, but it will grow. What's important is that he's a boyfriend. Ha ha, and boyfriends are important. I'll show people who I really am. They'll know who these guys are when I land up with one at school. No one's going to think I'm small little, sweet little Ruhi any more when I have a boyfriend who's in college. I'll be in every party pic then, won't I? No sudden silence when I appear at the lunch table, no switching topics to something safe. I'll be one of the cool kids. I text:

How about Friday?

My heart's somewhere in my throat. What am I doing? I can't go out and meet him. Delete. Delete.

Too late.

Friday's cool. I can bunk college

I can bunk school

What am I saying? I can't bunk school. I never have. Never in the past doesn't mean I can't in the future. Heart thuds.

Mumma walks in suddenly. 'Baby, Papa and I think you should go to the doctor. You've never been sluggish like this. Only, it's Sunday night, so doctors aren't easily available. Any other symptoms? Stomach pain?'

What? No. 'Yes, Mumma.' Anything to get her out of the room quick. Anything to not have to go sit and talk with them now.

The phone's lighting up. What's he saying?

Mumma's voice instead. 'Baby, stop studying so hard.' She comes over to my side and reaches over to shut the textbook.

'Leave me alone!' I twist the book away and see her face go pale.

'Ruhi? Baby, what happened?'

'I'm not a baby.' I want to lash out at her. I can't bear the disappointment in her eyes. I turn away and clutch my book to my stomach with the phone on page 114.

After what seems forever, I hear her leave. I hear her soft murmur to my father in the other room. They're so annoying, both of them, like one glued unit. We were all one unit, the three of us, a soldered three-point plug. Now it's them versus me. I'm not a baby, get used to it. I feel victorious. I feel awful.

Friday lunch at Pizza Pub at 1

I see the text. I send a thumbs-up.

He texts:

Can't wait to see you again

He texts:

Don't ditch

He texts:

You're awesome

He texts:

Remember the pic

He texts:

What a fantastic time we had

He texts:

Imagining us together

He texts:

Can't wait

I close my eyes.

ALISHA

Pull it together, Alisha, show them what you're made of. Stare at the red-plastic-framed mirror. Confront that girl with the raccoon eyeliner. There are streaks of it running down. Is this what you call pretty? Caved-in cheeks (I wish they were hollower; I wish I had cheekbones that stuck out like a supermodel's).

Turn on the tap and splash my face with water. Scrub at the eyeliner, the white foundation, the black lipstick. Rub rub rub at it till I wipe it all off, erase the face behind it too. If only.

Pull off the earrings, Alisha. Tear off the chains. Yank out the bracelets and bangles. Tug off the rings. The one with the red stone is stuck. It's from AK. As red as true love, he said. Eww! He didn't even know my finger size, so much for true love. It's too small. Too stuck. Stuck! Stuck! I'm too stuck! Panic rising, bile rising. Let the tap run and retch over the basin. Gargle. Rinse. Splash. Scrub. Peel off my black vest and black leggings. Stand under the cold shower till everything is washed away. Look at myself disappear, swirl out with the water – down into the plumbing pipes – away to the sea. Step out dripping wet. Pull on something lemony and cottony. Moni's pyjamas. Her sweatshirt too is hanging on the peg on the door. Big, white bear in a heart on the front. Get into it.

Replacement successful. Alisha out of the system, you people. Isn't that what you wanted? Here's a suitably average non-person instead.

I've deleted me.[20]

There's no one in my room when I walk out. I hear their voices from the living–dining area. Focus now – head held high, one foot in front of the other, in a straight line, walk out, eyes red but clear.

'Hi,' I announce in the sudden hush. 'I'm fine. Thanks.'

My father looks up. He wants to believe me, I can tell, but in the end, the other thing wins. He looks away. My mother just stares at me or through me or at someone she wants me to be. My uncle's wife jumps up from the dining chair, she comes over, arms outstretched in that forgiveness pose. Riti, she said to me when she first married into our family, no aunty and all required, after all, I'm only a few years older than you. Riti approaches.

I hold out a hand, palm up. Stall the attack. 'Chill! I've got exams from tomorrow. Going to study now. Goodnight, all.' I air-blow a kiss. 'Thanks again.'

Of course, *beti*.

Study well.

Goodnight.

Don't worry. You will be fine.

I close my room door behind me. Was that easy or what? Scamming the system. And one more thing – I *am* fine, you idiots. I am absolutely brilliant.

SHARAD

Sunday night has never dragged on so long. Thursday is forever and a half away. I can tell Tia to meet me tomorrow. I need my specs, I'll say. I can't see. I've got exams, I'll say. Nah, she'll see through it, specs or no specs. She's smart – and nice. She's got kind eyes. Slim eyes like – like long-grained Basmati rice. Yeeeah! That's not poetic. Well, she has. Unlike Alisha, whose eyes are like deep pools of – of, well, what? Of chlorinated water, what else is in a pool? Have to face it – am just not poetic. How am I going to ever charm a girl? Not by calling her eyes rice or chlorine, for sure.

Anyway, I've got my spare pair of specs on. Even nerdier than the previous ones. Really, I got to get them changed into something like that sporty stuff that Nihal wears. Will ask my mom for some money for a new pair. Why, she'll ask, what's wrong with these ones you have? I want sporty specs. But you don't play sports. But I'm going to. I'm trying for the javelin team. Hah, not with these arms, like she's going to believe me.

All right, Plan B. I need new spectacles because I lost mine. Truth and nothing but the truth. Where? At the party where this cute girl found them and is going to meet me over coffee to return them? Hmm, I don't think so.

Sudden realization. I need money. Need money to buy that coffee, forget the specs, sporty or not. How? I'll ask her for money to buy a new book – exam papers. Never fails. Sad to con her like this, but really, I'm only protecting her. She'd break out in a rash if I said I was dating. Or maybe not. What would she say?

How am I supposed to sleep with all these questions bouncing about in my head? I'll go down and walk around in the garden. Exercise releases relaxation hormones.

I make it downstairs and across the living room in the dark, without bumping into anything or stubbing my toe, proud of myself. The front door is open, huh? I step out and the cold takes my breath away. Now, that's lyrical. Girls' eyes don't do anything for my poetic senses, but weather does? I also feel an icy chill run up and down my spine. Positively writerly now… Only I turn around and see Cousinator#1, Kushal, sitting on one of the garden chairs. All alone – at least he was, till I came bumbling out. I turn to run back up, but it's too late, he's already staring at me. I wince, I'm going to get slaughtered now.

I start in a rush, 'You're probably wondering what I'm doing here in the middle of the night in the cold and not that I knew you were here, or I'd never have come and it's just that I had to because…' I stop. I've run out of gas. Out of ideas.

Kushal fixes me with that blank stare. In the dark. Like an owl. Maybe his head will rotate 180 degrees to the back now? Maybe he's got hypothermia, out here in the cold?

'I lost my main pair of specs,' I say finally. 'I thought I'd look for them here because, you know, I can't tell Maa because she would have to give me money for another pair and, you know, she doesn't really have her own money and I feel lousy and I don't know…'

He's pulling out something from the pocket of his kurta. Omigod, it's a gun. No, I watch way too many videos. It's a letter saying we've lost the house, all the millions, the business... No! It's a slim wad of notes. 'Don't ask her then,' he says.

I nod and take the notes. I can't believe my luck. Maybe the cold has seriously frozen his brain. I mean, why's he being nice?

He's the bad guy, right? Always has been. Never nice. Ever. People can't be both.[21]

There's got to be a catch, ya? I turn away, leaving him sitting there in the dark, and rush back upstairs. Back in my room, I wonder again what that was all about. And I remember that I didn't ask him why he was sitting alone in the dark. I didn't even thank him.

13

AK

Four days since the crash and everything still hurts. My arm. My ribs. Looking at Alisha hurts. Sitting in front of an exam paper, when I haven't really studied for it, hurts. But most of all, thinking hurts. Thinking of the closed doors at home. The wrecked car. My dad's face.

Alisha has been acting like nothing's wrong.

Sure, she'd looked shocked on Monday morning, while walking to class, when she saw my arm in a cast. 'What's with that?' she drew up alongside me. I was freaking mad at her for ghosting me. Had she come with me that night, I would have been more careful, I wouldn't have crashed. This was all her fault. And not answering my calls when I was lying there, bleeding to death – well, almost, who knows, I might have…

I shrugged and that set off ripples of jabbing pain.

'Oh,' she said, 'does it hurt?'

Does it? Fractured arm in plaster, scratches across my cheek. I turned away from her. 'Nah!' I said, 'Nothing hurts me.' Point taken, Al? Not even you.

She looked at me strangely and walked away.

Yes. Everything is agony. Even watching her walk away. Especially that.

Everyone had heard about my accident, naturally, and so that Monday morning, they soon clustered around me. For the first ten minutes, I felt like a god once more. I went over the accident again and again, for each person who asked me, each time making it sound a bit scarier, a little more thrilling, the sounds louder – the crash into the tree, my head whipping around, my arm twisting, biting down the pain till my lips bled, beads of cold sweat drenching my collar, the wrenching of my gut (all this borrowed from a book I'd read).

'And then I pulled him out,' came Sharad's voice from somewhere at the back of the crowd.

'You?'

'Wow!'

'Really?'

And the crowd parted, so I was looking at him, his eyebrows raised, challenging me.

'Yeah, he pulled me out,' I mumbled.

'I saved you,' Sharad said pointedly.

'He saved me,' I had to admit, glaring at him.

The bell rang. The crowd scattered. Exams took over.

I waved off the teacher who had offered to help me write the papers. So here I am, plodding through the exams with my brain dulled, but everything else supersensitive: back, head, ribs, arm, and the heart I pretend not to have.

SHARAD

Only W-e-d-n-e-s-d-a-y! Can't believe Thursday is still not here. It's taking a month of Sundays to arrive, isn't it? Though my math-brain can't wrap itself around that phrase. It's only Wednesday – one whole day more to go. And three days of mind-numbing exams over, which I could have sailed through with my eyes closed. And probably did too – have been spending so many nights awake, making up conversations with Tia, at least a hundred-odd variations that will end with her in my arms. Oh, need to buy deo too!

Tomorrow evening at four at the café where she works after school. Only I've been walking past it every evening, trying to spy on her. Spot her, I mean. Anyway, the stupid glass panes in the café reflect everything off the street, so I can only see myself peering in most of the time. I hope she hasn't seen me. And the counter is way up at the back, so I have to try to look past the tables and chairs and heads and – why do people drink so much coffee? Can't they go and jog around the park or something so I have a clear view across empty tables? But then, her café won't have so much business and she won't have a job and… Not that I'm a stalker. I leave every evening after my first glance of her.

On Monday, she was carrying a tray (again? – this is how I'm going to picture her for the rest of my life), and on Tuesday, she walked too close to the glass front and I had to bend over immediately to tie a shoelace on a shoe that had none. And when I finally straightened up from tying the non-existent laces of my non-laced shoes, with a crick in my back, she was taking the order from a guy who said something to make her laugh. Her head thrown back, curls bouncing wildly, made me want to dash in and dunk his stupid face into his coffee, and there really should be rules against patrons flirting with people who are working hard to try and earn a living. I should start an online campaign.

And today, I can't see her, though I've walked past the café so often that the guy selling phone covers on the pavement is looking at me, alarmed. He keeps shielding his display every time I get close to him. And then, suddenly, when I've almost melted into the glass pane wondering if she's on leave today, her face pops up from inside, right in front of me. And she grins and signals me in. And I'm so startled that I turn back immediately towards the phone-cover seller.

'How much for this one?'

'For which model?' he asks, taken aback.

'I don't know. It's not important.'

'All covers don't fit all phones,' insists this idiot salesman, who seems wired towards not selling instead of the opposite.

'Just give me that blue one, it will fit.'

'Single cover or double – like a folder?'

'Single. Double. Quick!'

'Where is your phone? Let me see where the camera is.' He holds out his hand.

I jab my hand into my pocket, when he suddenly says, 'Yes, tell me, do you want a phone cover?' Again? Is he on some recorded loop? I look up sharply, but he's looking over my shoulder and I turn around like in that slow-mo thing you see on screen – and of course, it's Tia standing there.

'Come on in,' she tells me. 'You're really bad for business, scaring our patrons by squashing yourself against the glass pane.'

'I thought he looked suspicious too – these days, you really don't know who is who,' offers the phone-cover dude.

ALISHA

Only a few know that the door to the terrace above the block that's being renovated is usually left open. It looks out on the back wall of the school, and from there you can see a skyline of haphazardly built houses, a small set of open fields, some mounds of sand on an abandoned construction site, and lanes that could probably allow a car in, if it were willing to drive over a few flowerpots or toes.

The terraces in school are out of bounds, and their doors locked. This one's open, I suspect, because a teacher or student or cook or guard hops over here to have a secret smoke. It's against the rules to smoke on campus, and this place is littered with butts.

I often escape here, after class, to the fifth floor, above the drone of voices below.

Keep your head held high, Alisha. The ground is filled with buzzing bees and narrow corridors and constricting rules, but up here, it's open. The sky is endless… Stretch out your arms. Close your eyes. Fly.

A yelp carries over. Lean over, Alisha, over the wall, and there's that sandpit with a litter of newborn pups you've been watching for days now. Look how fast they're growing up. Slow down, little ones. Look at them scramble over each other, biting, yelping. They're gorgeous. There's the mother running over with something in her mouth for them. They leap at her, delirious with joy. She lets them suckle, giving each a good lick over. So much love out there.

So little out here.

Don't you have a heart, Alisha? Can't you love AK back the way he wants you to? He doesn't ask for much. What about that sweet little thing – Ruhi? She worships you. Look at her. Talk to her. No? What about your parents? Feel nothing for them?

Love's overhyped. It's just a marketing gimmick. I'm not going to fall for it.[22]

What about your entire brood of relatives, Alisha? They are trying to reach out to you. Don't you care? Your sister Moni…

Stop! Not Moni! Leave her out of this.

RUHI

Three days of school over and two to go for the Twilight date. Time's flying. I wish I could make it stop. I wish it would happen quickly already. No, I wish it would not. I wish I'd wake up and discover that I'm only dreaming. But it *is* a dream. Every girl's dream. He's gorgeous-looking, that stubble, that – can't remember much more of what he looked like.

For the first time ever, I can't focus on my exams. They're just going on and on…

Only midway through the week. And every exam so far has been fully forgettable. I'm sure I'll get by with so-so marks. I can't do badly even if I try, right? Good girls always win in the end. Seen it in a million movies.

I'm leaving school among the usual high-pitched shrieks and babbling; everyone comparing answers, pages flapping – see, this was the right answer, told you so! And all that. Usually, I'd be in the middle of it all, but today I'm just staring out at the sky. Dark clouds emerging – could that mean rain will follow? Will it pour on Friday? Then, surely, I can't be expected to meet anyone. I mean, it could be flooded by then. Or storming and – who goes out when there's thunder and lightning? That's just unsafe. Good girls don't do unsafe things.

What's that over there? Omigod, there's someone on top of that building, the one that they're rebuilding, some idiot standing, arms stuck out. Like a lightning conductor – no one goes there – it's so at the back of beyond. Oh no, they – he – she – is leaning over the wall – going to jump? I bite back a scream.

Wild-eyed, I turn around and grab at the first person I find near me. It's that massive tree-trunk, AK, Alisha's boyfriend, ex-boyfriend, whatever. 'Help! Someone's jumping,' I say hoarsely. He looks at me, puzzled. We've barely spoken to each other even though we've been together since kindergarten. He's on another trip, another league, another circle, another cloud.

I point out feebly towards the terrace of that block – the one with rubble. 'Someone's jumping – help!' I repeat desperately.

His eyes shift to over my head and beyond. I turn to look. There's no one there.

Did the person jump? Was I hallucinating? Am I having a breakdown? Should I insist on someone going to check? Or do I need help myself?

'Sorry,' I mumble.

14

SHARAD

I follow Tia sheepishly into the café. She points to a smallish round table right at the back, by the kitchen door. It is covered with printouts, files, labels and stuff. It's where the staff works, I deduce.

'Wait here,' she says. I clamber over a few cartons to get to the chair squashed into the corner. She goes to the counter and brings over three stacks of bills, skewered down their middles on three sharp spikes. 'If you help me count these, I can get away earlier. But if you'd rather stare at phone covers or hug glass…' She trails off, straight-faced. She must be smiling on the inside. I bet she's smiling on the inside. I'm leaping and frolicking on the inside.

In my eagerness to show off my superior mental math skills, I fly through the bills, adding numbers at the speed of light. I run through the first stack and do a cross-check – different totals. Arrrrhhh! Again. Totally different total. Again. Off by a few hundreds this time. I grab the calculator on the table and start all over. Tia is back. 'We can pay you in coffee. Have you done all three?'

I hang my head miserably – I'm still halfway through the first. 'I'm really brilliant at math, ask my classmates – I am,' I say.

Tia places a cup of foamy coffee on the table, edging the bills aside. 'Just wanted to keep you busy. We've got programs to do this stuff. Computer age and all.'

I blink at her.

Tia perches on one of the cartons. 'Got a friend to cover for me for half an hour.'

I don't even know how to start, now that I'm sitting here on a real live date with a real live girl. Luckily, I don't have to. Tia seems to have no such hang-ups. She's saying, 'So I feel like I know you already.'

'Uh?'

'You tie shoelaces you don't have, buy phone covers you don't want and stalk girls you know nothing about.'

I must have looked startled because she says quickly, 'Not me. That pretty one at the party. The one you're clearly crazy about.'

'Alisha,' I say finally, and then I go to much trouble to explain to her why I was following Alisha, what I thought it would be like and how it wasn't quite like what I thought it would be and...basically I spend the first precious minutes of my date talking about another girl. I constantly amaze myself!

I stop. 'I'm sorry,' I say. 'Research shows it takes less than five minutes when we first talk to someone to decide whether we like them or not. I've lost my first five minutes, haven't I?'

'Yes,' Tia says. 'But I'm wildly interested now in what else research says.'

'About?'

'About the people you meet at parties?'

I look down.

'I'll tell you,' Tia leans forward and looks me in the eye. 'I waitress because I want to earn my own money. The lady who owns this café – she knows this, and she pays me decently. I work here after school hours and on weekends, and then make some more money if I go to parties that we cater for.'

She stops and looks at my face intently.

I say, 'I'd like to earn too. Could I get a job here?'

'Are your baking skills as brilliant as your math skills?'

We're laughing. I'm in love. Obviously. Research says teens keep falling in love with everyone – someone who looks their way on a bus, or someone in a magazine. But...

It's easy to talk to her. She asks me why I want to work. I tell her I'm an only kid with a single mom. Tia tells me they're three siblings with a single mom. She wins, she claims, grinning.

She's stunningly open about her life. 'My dad was my hero. He was a manager in a tea garden in Assam, where he met my mom who was a doctor there. He died when my younger bro was just a year old.' I wish

I could do more. I want to reach out and place my hand over hers, but I am guessing she isn't looking for sympathy. She's obviously at a place where she can talk about who she is and where she's coming from. I'm the one who's not. And besides, if I try to touch her hand, she'd probably slap me.

She asks, 'So when did your dad die?'

A painful, embarrassed silence. Almost a minute passes.

'He didn't,' I say.

It's the first time I've told anyone this.

Whenever someone asked, I'd invent heroic and tragic deaths for my father, ones that made his leaving us seem less like our fault.

I feel the familiar darkness threaten to pull me under, but I hear her say, 'Time up! Poingggg!' How's she so cheerful despite the lousy hand she's been dealt? Despite a full day at school and then working at this café?

How can someone who's been knocked down so badly, still bounce back? Am I still talking about her? Or me?[23]

She's a mind reader, clearly, because she says, 'I'm sad for our family. But I'm also proud of us.'

Tia stands up and fetches a take-home paper bag from the counter, which she wiggles at me. I open it to find my spectacles inside.

'Thanks,' I say, taking my cue to leave. I'm thanking her for much more than just my specs.

I'm at my bus stop by the time the ping I expected, arrives.

Hey, u left ur cap here

I have my reply ready:

Oh. Now I got 2 be here tom again. I'll b tying my laces outside till UR free

RUHI

Friday's here, 1 p.m. is here. And I'm here. At Pizza Pub. Black tights, white kurti. It took me fifty minutes and thirteen changes of clothes to choose this last night. Not too much, not too little. Definitely not as little as that little black skirt. That hated black skirt. I twisted it into a ball and shoved it into the back of my shoe rack. Never want to see it again. It was so pretty once upon a time.

This is better. More appro-pri-ate! Sends out the right signals. Well covered. But cute. Of course, I couldn't go out dressed like this because I was supposed to go to school, so I left home in my uniform like any other day, hugging and waving to Mumma-Papa, lugging my lunch box. Only, I skipped the bus and Uber-ed it to the mall instead, where I spent an hour in the restroom pulling out clothes and shoes from my school bag, and folding my uniform back in, combing out my plaits so that my hair tumbled in waves down my back, applying the red lipstick, then washing it off. The other women who walked in and out of the restroom threw me telling side glances. One began to say something. I fixed her with a glare, and she just offered me a smile instead and turned away. Mind your own business, y'all! I know what I'm doing. Even if I don't. This lipstick doesn't work.

I wandered around the mall, pulling clothes off racks and trying them out. I bought a black lipstick with the emergency money Mumma stashes in my hidden pocket. If black lipper makes Alisha look like Alisha, then it's good for me, yeah! I kept going to the fourth-floor food court to look out through the glass panes, across the street at Pizza Pub. Obviously, the people eating at the tables near the window had to move aside to allow me to stick myself against the glass, and they weren't too thrilled about it – but who cares about them? Not the new Ruhi, no.

At 12:45, I was in Pizza Pub, in the booth at the back, facing the door, black tights and black lipstick – pulling my white kurti down to cover my knees. I was feeling sick, my face was slick with sweat, my heart was beating somewhere in my throat, my palms were clammy. I wanted to run away and go home. I wanted to stay.

It's a self-service place, so luckily no waiter would come over to hover around me.

At 1 p.m., it's a no-show. After a couple of minutes, I stand up and pick up my school bag to leave, when I spot the door swing open. A guy stands silhouetted in the bright light from outside. He has a hunky jacket on. I duck back into the booth and pretend to be madly engrossed in my phone.

After a few minutes, I look up. No one walks over to me. Can't he see me? Did he see me and decide I didn't look cute enough in the daylight? OMG! Embarrassing! I do look cute, give me a chance. I shake my head, so that my hair swings around my shoulders like a shampoo ad. I bite my lips, and my eyes dart around the pub frantically. There is an office team at a table in the centre, a few other tables with groups of threes and fours, and a scattering of couples – and there – right across the room is the guy with the jacket, back to me, sitting in a booth, with some random girl. My breath gets caught somewhere in my chest. No, this can't be happening. He said he liked me. He said he keeps thinking about me. How many other girls has he invited to the pub? This is the shortest first love in history. He turns his head, and I see he's someone totally different. Oh!

It's 1:25 and I think I'm being stood up. I should leave. Keep my dignity. I don't need to hang around for any guy. No one else defines me. I stand up. I sit down. I will wait till 1:30 and only till then. After all, he has my picture – that's blackmail. I hate him. And when he lands up, I'll tell him just how much I detest him. In no uncertain terms. I will use the language I hear other kids use in school, all those words. I'm no baby.

It's 1:30.

It's 1:55. I feel like crying. My love affair has ended even before it began. I feel stupid. I look down at my phone – he hasn't even messaged. I feel totally teary.

'Hi, baby.' I squint up and he's looming over me, as handsome as I remember. Even though, honestly, I was too high on that spiked-coke-thing to really remember. 'Hope you weren't waiting too long. The traffic…' He lets it trail off as he squeezes into my bench, not in all the tonnes of space across from me.

'No, no…I was running so late myself. I just got here. I thought you'd be gone,' I rush on. I lie so easily. Me. Papa would be so disappointed – they always told me to be truthful. Stop thinking of Mumma-Papa now. Twilight is saying something. Can't keep calling him Twilight. But how can I ask him his name so late in our relationship. Look, he's already got his arm slung around the back of our seat, with his hand cupped around my shoulder. This is what it feels like to be held. It's nice.

'You're even cuter than I remember,' he says, sliding his hand through my hair. I think of Mumma brushing my hair. I push the thought away.

'So are you,' I reply. Truth. Because I don't remember.

On that note, yeah, gotta ask him now…and I do, *verrrrry* casually, 'By the way, that pic you took of us. Let me see?'

'Sure,' he pats his pocket and his face falls. 'Oh, sorry, baby, it's on my other phone. Left that at home. Anyway, who needs a pic when I've got the real thing here.' He gives me a hug and I sorta let the pic slip out of my mind.

We spend almost two hours there, him talking about movies, and bikes, which I know nothing of, but he goes on about forever. I do a lot of nodding and smiling and not much eating of that pizza. I insist I hardly eat, which of course is a roaring lie, because I love to eat. I just pretend I am Alisha, scoffing at the food, pushing my single slice of pizza around my plate. He does a lot of playing with my hair, rubbing my shoulder, my knee, throwing his head back and laughing, nuzzling my neck. I do a lot of laughing too, and throwing my head back. It makes my hair swish.

I know about consent, okay?! I wasn't born yesterday. I'm not dumb. I chose this. I want this. Right? Why is it so tough to convince myself then that I like this? I mean, he keeps saying he likes me. Nothing wrong with wanting to be liked. Plus, it's seriously high time I got myself someone special. I'll grow to love him. He's really handsome, with this stubble and gelled hair and those almost-white eyes – grey? Silver? I'm a lucky girl.

'How did you get away on a school day?' he asks at some point.

'I am the captain of my fate, I am the master of my soul,' I quote. His brow furrows and I mumble, '*Invictus*.'

'Yeah, of course, great movie!' he smiles.

I smile back. Loving someone means accepting everything about them, even if they don't – sigh – read. Finally, I say, 'I've got to be home before the school bus, and I've got to get changed back into my uniform too.' I gesture at my tights and laugh.

'I'd like to see you in your uniform,' he leans in. 'And maybe take a few more pics. Like the one I have, remember?'

And then suddenly, I am falling – through thin ice into the water below – and it's cold. Freezing.

15

ALISHA

I want to be anywhere else. Anywhere but here. Last week dragged like a broken leg. Exams at school. And at home, my parents checking on me while pretending they were not. This week's been even duller. Boring! Bleh! AK acting like I don't exist. I stand on the terrace, sometimes I even climb on to the wall. I want to close my eyes and be somewhere else. Anywhere else.

Think, Alisha, you've got one of the best brains around. You know this. You want to get away, you can. What about Moni then? She'll be fine. She'll be finer without you, Alisha.

Focus on getting away. Where? How? You need money to get away, to go somewhere, get a job, pretend you're twenty – that'll be easy to pull off. Live alone, live an exciting life, do what you want, no one telling you what to eat or wear and no one waiting at home to see what time you actually get back. No one spying. Pretending they care. You don't need anyone. Well, except now.

I look down and see the usual ruckus, kids pouring out of the gates after the last bell. Running home like they – like they – why would they want to get home? Sharad's weaving in and out of the crowd – he sure seems to be in a hurry. Sharad. Of course! Sharad! He'll help me. Of course. He's putty, clay-doh, malleable.

I run to the terrace door and charge down the flights of stairs. By the time I get to the school gate, he is turning the corner of the street. I run. Me running after Sharad, funny or what? There he is at the bus stop. I slow down to catch my breath. I can't be seen puffing and – frantic. Even if I am, right now. Slow down, Alisha, stay cool.

Hey, stop! He's getting on a bus. What? No! I make a dash for it too, but it's too far off.

The people at the bus stop are staring at my athletic flop show. What are you gawking at? Morons! Not like anyone would help. Not like anyone stopped the bus when they saw me trying to catch it. Not like anyone ever helps.

'You can take the next bus to Domlur, it will come in seven minutes,' an old man says, nodding at me.

Okay, take that back. A bit. Someone helps. Sometimes. Just once in a while. That's all. I mutter something, looking down, which I mean to be a thank you. That's big coming from me. And we all stand silently after that, while the minutes tick by, and I can finally hop on to the bus he points out to me.

I haven't really thought this through. Where will Sharad get off? How will I catch up with him? All I know is that I've got to get out of here. Get out of this place, it's suffocating me. Get out of my life, my skin. And it's got to be today. Now.

SHARAD

Okay, it's official. I'm in love and it's not like all that swooning over unattainable dream girls that I used to be so good at. It's official; we're a thing. Tia and me. We've met every day since that corny meeting at the café. All through the rest of the exam week, and now, we're almost through the next. In the park that has become our go-to place to hang out. Student budgets don't really allow restaurant romances. So we pick up a boiled-to-death cup of tea in a paper cup from the *paan-dukaan* and then sip at it while we sit in the park. We make that micro-cup of tea last an hour or two. Magic! And not just the tea, hah!

Until you can manage time, you can manage nothing else, says Peter Drucker on my wall. Not even you, Mr Drucker, can manage time like I can.

Here I am again. I have just put my backpack down on a bench, annoyed that our usual bench is taken by this other couple who have nothing better to do at five in the evening than to sit and moon over each other in a park. Yes, I'm aware of the irony, thank you. But seriously, go stare at each other somewhere else, won't you?

'Sharad!' I hear the voice and there is something off about it. I turn around to look over the hedge and see someone waving at me as she walks through the gate.

I know I have imagined this moment many, many times before. So there's a sense of déjà vu as she slow-mos over to me, a smile on her radiant face, her skirt swishing around those long legs. The one girl I'd spent forever dreaming about. Alisha.

ALISHA

I push out of the stifling crowds at the teeming Domlur bus stand without a clue about where I should go. Step out into the street, Alisha, and let your legs just take you. The street slides past residences, shops, gyms, a park. And in between the tall ferns that border the park, I glimpse Sharad sliding into a bench. Like a had-to-happen scene from a movie. I've never been so excited to see him. Ever. The stars have not let me down. The pieces are all falling into place. This is meant to be, Alisha. You're on your way. Out of here.

'Sharad!' I call. He flips his head my way, surprised. I wave and squeeze in through the gate, walk over and sit down beside him.

The equation's changed subtly. I'm not listening to that voice in my head, the dark, guarded, manipulative one. Instead there's a sort of rewind. All the times Sharad came through for me. Whenever I needed a friend. This dude's been the one constant in my life, always there for me. I let my defences drop as I hear myself saying, in a gush, 'Sharad, I need to talk to you. Yeah, I followed you here. You're the only one who can help me. I need to get away. This place sucks. You know that too. Actually, we can both go, escape – you and me. Far away from here.'

There! Let myself speak for once without planning each word and its impact. I look at this person whom I've been playing around with, making him dance around like a cursor on a screen. And I see him as kind, not weak. Why did I ever think he was weak? He's smart, I'm strong, we can help each other. We'll take on the world and whatever it has in store for us. I'm on a rush. 'Come with me,' I say. 'Let's get out of here, out of this place, this school, this city. We can do anything we want. Imagine, Sharad…'

I see a light flick on in his eyes, and then fade away. He says nothing. The next time he looks at me, it isn't at me, he's looking over my shoulder. I swivel around and see a curly-haired girl standing with a paper cup in her hand. There's something vaguely familiar about her. She grins. 'Hi,' she says. 'Hi, Alisha. I'm Tia.'

SHARAD

I'm dreaming, right? Tell me I'm dreaming. Look at me. Do I look like the kind of dude who has two gorgeous girls hanging out with him? I should pinch myself. While I sit in a trance, the girls are saying something I should probably be paying attention to.

Alisha is turning red, flustered, saying, 'I'm sorry.'

Tia is chuckling, 'And I'm Tia.'

'How do you know me? Who are you?'

'I'm Tia. The third time I've said that. From the party. I was waitressing. May I sit? The tea's hot.'

And then I think it's time I say something too. And that pendulum – swinging between the girl of my dreams and – well, Tia – it has stopped.

Choices. Choices. It all boils down to choices.[24]

Tia has squeezed in on the other side of me. I put my arm around her shoulder, and it's the first time I've done that. She lets me. I clear my throat and do one of the things I never imagined I would do. I close the door on Alisha.

'This. Is. Tia,' I say. Fourth time, yup. 'She. Me.' I don't need to carry on. English Ma'am would be aghast. Verbless, grammarless, sentenceless communication. But still, it works.

There is something decisive about that arm-around-the-shoulder thing. I see it in Alisha's eyes. She backs up suddenly, jumping to her feet. 'I've – I've got to go. I – Sharad – ignore whatever I just said.' She looks at Tia for a longish moment and then sashays off. I look at her walk away. B'bye, dream girl.

Tia slurps the tea. 'Bye-bye, dream girl!' She's a mind reader, this one. She grins. 'If I were a guy, I'd have chosen her over me.'

She hands me the cup and I take a long sip. I'm ridiculously happy all of a sudden. 'I'm glad you're not a guy.'

It sounds blah, I know, but it was one sweet moment. And not just the three spoons of sugar per cup.

RUHI

'All of it?'

I'm sitting in Style. That's the salon in my neighbourhood with the glossy glam pics of pink-tinted spiky-haired women covering the entire window. Of course no one in my neighbourhood ever gets their hair done like that. No one ever comes to Style except for 'trim the split ends off'. The girls in mauve aprons who sit and thread each other's eyebrows are all clustered around me. Because this is the most shocking request they've ever had.

'All of it?' the lady with the scissors asks again. She's asked twice already in rising levels of disbelief. 'All of it? Are you sure? Do your parents know?'

'Yes – all,' I say, facing the mirror. I want to look at each step of this decision I'm making. It's taken the longest few days of my life to get me to this point. Oscillating between Twilight's pledges of love and thinly veiled threats. But I'm here now.

Half an hour later, I stand up, dusting off my shoulders, and nod at the girl in the mirror. Me. As I've never known me before. My hair has been cropped down to a centimetre off my scalp. Almost bald.

Mumma can't spend ages brushing my long hair and braiding her warnings about bad girls into it. Twilight can't run his hands through the luxuriant tresses and tell me how beautiful I'd look in the kind of pictures he wants to take of me, the kind that would make me famous online – beautiful pictures of me covered with only my beautiful hair.

16

AK

The collapse of my world begins with scrambled eggs.

That's what I'm having after school. Jaggu Kaka's been fussing over me, I think he'd hand-feed me if he could, because of my sling and all. I'm not protesting because – hey – I need some TLC after the lousiest days of my life. It couldn't get worse.

And then it does.

I'm alone at the gleaming marble-topped table for eight. Heavy maroon drapes shut out any sunshine that dares peep into our dining room. The fountain in the corner keeps a steady gurgle going. Some jingle that's supposed to be soothing. Annoying as hell. Rajasthani paintings on silk at exactly two feet apart, stretch out across one wall, elongated women with mirror-work heads and eyes that are permanently averted. Very over the top, our décor, considering we paid some interior design company a fortune to get it to look understated.

I'm saying all this because the fountain, the mirrors, the women in the paintings are mute witnesses to my collapsing world.

Jaggu Kaka is patting my shoulder with his 'One more toast, come on' and 'Look how weak you have become, have butter at least' and 'Why have you stopped drinking milk? Too old now? How will your bones grow?' I nod absently while flipping through the news on my phone.

Thursday evening breaking news. Apocalypse headlines, what's new about that? Multi-crore–rupee construction scam. Builder on the run. Many houseowners lose their savings. To sue...criminal proceedings...'my savings for my retirement,' says ex-army man...bad loans...lawyer demands that...

The builder on the run holds his hand up to hide his face in the image.

The builder.

On the run.

In the multi-crore scam.

Is my dad.

The toast and eggs choke in my throat. I look around desperately. At the closed bedroom doors. Where's my mom? Where's my sister? Don't they know? Is this true? How can this be happening? My dad may be hot-tempered, drunk, aggressive. But he's not corrupt, not dishonest, not twisted. No. He's my hero. He's the man I have tried all my life to become.

I stagger to my father's room and bang on the door. I've got to get him to tell me it's not true. To make it go away. Jaggu Kaka's hurrying behind me, trying to hold me back. I push the door open and he's not there. Of course not. He's the builder on the run.

Nothing makes sense. Everything makes sense. Have I always known this about him? Of course not. I've never suspected this. Or have I? My life's been built on lies. Lies that I've told myself. I've been a fool.

I see everything through a red haze. I begin to throw things, expensive things – at other expensive things. I throw my father's golf trophy at the wall – it hits one of the framed paintings and shatters the glass. I lob my plate at a door. More splintering. The mug against the sideboard. The photo frame against the fountain. At least, that silences that mind-numbing jingle. The dogs go into a frenzy of nervous barking. So not the peace and quiet of Home Sweet Home. I want to break more than just glass, I want to break this illusion, this pricey fake bubble I live in. I only stop when I realize that Jaggu Kaka is the one who will have to clean up after me. I'm terrifying him and the dogs.

'So you've found out?' My mom stands framed in her doorway in a red satin kimono or kaftan or whatever it's called. One closed door has opened at least.

'Found out?' I'm screaming. Pacing restlessly. Livid. 'That means you knew all along? And you're *okay* with this?' I see myself in the mirror. King Kong.

'Sit!' she says, settling into a dining chair. 'And don't scream. The neighbours can hear you.'

'I don't care!' I shout louder. I slam my fist on the table.

Simone whimpers and my mom picks her up on to her lap. 'Sit down!' she tells me.

I don't sit. I don't buy this crap any more. No more illusions. No more cover-ups. No more lies. 'Mom. Is this true?'

She keeps stroking Simone while I keep ranting, 'Is this true? Is it? Is it?'

I know it is. Finally, I run out of steam and sit. 'Has he really run off with all those people's money?'

'They say he has.'

'You must have known, Mom. All these years. He couldn't have suddenly turned twisted.'

'He's a businessman. He's done deals he's had to. We've enjoyed the good things that those deals buy. I'm not condoning it. I'm not part of it. But I've watched it happen.'

I cannot get myself to agree. 'You are part of it. Turning a blind eye is helping him cover up.'

'It's more complicated than that. He's been a good father to you and your sister. In return, I've been a good wife. I've stayed by his side.'

I want to barf. I cannot take this. I cannot belong to these two people. I cannot have their twistedness running through my veins. I have to be bigger than this. I don't realize how much it's become about me till I hear my mother say, 'This is about your father. You are not him.'

I look at her and notice her face for the first time in years, really, really see her, you know. I see the puffy purple circles under her eyes, the wrinkles pulling down the mouth, the jaunty pink lipstick she's never seen without. I want to hurt her, I want to lash out and make her feel as ripped-up inside as I am. I can feel the salty taste of tears and I want her to see them. 'How do you face yourself in the mirror, Mom? How do you not hate yourself?'

She flinches but keeps on looking at me, her chin still raised. 'I did what I had to. I do. To give you both decent lives. Don't judge me. Why do you think I do these unending charity drives? It wasn't just to "tick the boxes". Some part of me feels like I'm doing something good, giving back…like I'm helping to restore the balance…'

'You're justifying it. Excuses! I hate you. I hate you both. I hate this house.'

'Well, you won't be living here much longer, if that makes you feel any better. The courts will probably attach our properties and other assets to recover the loans, you should know that.' She lifts Simone and places her in the basket with the other two dogs, and chin still raised, back straight, she turns and walks back into her room.

I notice then that Neo has been standing there silently, leaning against the door frame of her room. None of her usual biting wit. She walks over, drags the basket with the three spaniels into her room. 'They'll cut their paws to ribbons on all this broken glass.' She shuts her door, walks back and squats on the floor next to Jaggu Kaka, who is now busy with a dustpan and stick broom. I get down beside him, to pick the shards of glass out of the carpet with my one functional hand. The three of us work quietly, but gradually I stop sobbing.

The day the world collapses is the day I see my parents for who they actually are. Not super-successful superheroes. But human – and weak humans at that.

No good at even being human.

What does that make me now?

When I don't want to be my father any more.[25]

RUHI

The first thing I do when I get out of the salon is send Twilight a pic of me with my close-cropped pate:

Bald as a table-tennis ball

What? Why?

His reply is instant. Victory, I think. I've won.

Smiling, I text:

Guess no more pics now. No more long hair

No response, till I'm almost home.

Bald chicks are hawt! The photo session is so ON!!

SHARAD

My mother is a goddess. My cousins are pillars. My classmates are angels. My teachers are heroes. My uncles' house is paradise. The nerdy spectacles are lifesavers. And all because of one fabulous, hot, brilliant, fun, amazing... (Running out of adjectives here, something I never do – given how long I've spent mugging up the thesaurus in my quest to crack the entrance exams.)

Every evening, I've been hugging my mother, high-fiving any gobsmacked cousin I come across before he has time to say something snarky. I've sat through my aunt's rant in the kitchen about something I had no clue about – was it the rocketing price of onions? Or the inefficiency of call-centre staff? I couldn't care less, except she ended by hugging me and telling me she wished her own sons cared like I did.

The sky is full of rainbows and the sun is chirping and the birds are shining – and I'm not high on anything except love and fresh air. Even though everyone's complaining that the air quality in the city sucks.

This evening, back after meeting Tia, I float into my mother's room. I might even have done a pirouette, but don't hold me to that. 'So are you going to tell me why you're acting so strange lately?' My mother looks up from the pyjamas she is darning.

'Just like that!' I hold her face between my hands and plant a kiss on her forehead.

'Topped your class?' she hazards a guess.

'No.'

'Cracked a quiz?'

'No.'

'Won an award?'

'No.'

She goes through the list of usual suspects. The stuff that I've struggled to achieve. Working on a project? No. Written a code for an app that's featured somewhere? No. Got an article published? No. Heard from a professor at a college I'm keen on? No.

'It must be something. You've been coming home so late every evening. Extra classes? Wait! Have you got an internship? Is that the surprise?'

I sit next to her, take the needle from her hand and tell her, 'I've met a girl.'

My mother has spent so long keeping herself tough, her emotions veiled, her face non-committal – that even I can't read her. I look into her eyes, behind specs as thick as my own.

Finally, she smiles, 'Tell me about her.'

I curl into a childhood pose, my head in her lap while she ruffles my hair, and I do.

I tell her about Tia.

17

ALISHA

Days pass. Blank calendar pages flipping past. Almost two weeks since that party, two weeks full of nothing. I can barely remember what day it is today. Friday? Weekend coming up. Weekend full of emptiness.

I have nothing inside me either. I've emptied it all out. Every last bit. Empty. No food. No strength. No anger. No dreams.

Class is over for the day, kids rampaging around, everyone's lives filled with chatter, laughter, something to look forward to. Mine is empty.

The sun is so harsh today. Stand up on that terrace wall, Alisha. Feel on top of the world again. Like the bird you are. Bird of prey. But I can't, because there's no one left to prey on. Depend on. Not even Sharad.

Why is everything outside swimming today? As far as my eyes can see – haze. The buildings are wavy, the trees a blur, the sand piles underwater. The sun's so hot. I've got nothing inside me. I'm air. I'm falling.

RUHI

If you want to know how powerful something is, get rid of it.

My hair, my choice, right? Wrong! Cutting one tree has destroyed the entire forest. It is everyone's concern.

What hurt the most was not cutting the hair off. Dead cells. It was going home from the salon yesterday to Mumma opening the door and her silent cry of horror. Later, Papa came in to sit in my room, his eyes swimming – What did we do wrong, Baby?

I'm hurting, I wanted to say. It's not you. It's me. It's my hair. It's pictures of me with my beautiful hair and nothing else, that I wanted to cut off. So that they wouldn't hurt you. I was trying to protect you, not hurt you, I wanted to say. I'm growing up. I'm making decisions now. My own.

Breaking out of a cocoon hurts. But I still need to. I need to flex my own wings now.[26]

And today, I took my new look to school. Gasps all around, of course. I'd played goddesses in annual day plays and every epitome of flawless girlhood on stage on every occasion. Flowing hair framing an expression of frozen purity.

My classmates reacted and how. Whoa! What? Wow! No way! What happened? Is that for real? So sorry! Are you okay? But why? Hey, that's so cool!

Never has little Ruhi been so much the centre of attraction. Class is over, though, and it's time to head back home. I refill my water bottle and walk down the corridor, looking out at the horizon – and there's that figure again. On the terrace. I stop and watch. The person climbs up on to the wall and holds out wing-like arms. And. Falls.

I hold back a scream.

Am I seeing things? Stress? Should I just go back home and forget I saw this? No. I can't. But I must. I have enough problems of my own. And how do I even get to that terrace? I should tell someone. No one will believe me. Let me pretend I never saw that.

SHARAD

She's here. Tia. Waiting for me at the crossroads. Is there a song like that? There should be. I should write it. For her. Wait for me at the crossroads and wherever we go, we'll go together. Corny. Lyrics have got to be a bit eww, anyway. All of them are.

I'm bursting with my Tia secret. No one's ever gonna believe she's my girl. I'm dying to have her wait outside the gate and, as the kids pour out, we'll go running into each other's arms, eyes locked. With that song playing in the background. The one I'm going to write. With the cheesy lyrics.

But for now, she's waiting at the crossroads near the park…

I've got to get her to meet Maa first. It's the decent thing to do by her. Who her? Tia. And Maa. I'm a gentleman like that. Brought up well. Some day, I'll get Maa and her together. Some day when the time's right.

She's in her school uniform today because she's taken an evening off from the café. She hasn't changed into that apron thingie yet. She's wearing a white blouse and a grey pleated skirt, white keds with double-bow-knotted laces. She's got a smiley drawn with a pink pen on one.

'Stop staring!' Tia swings her backpack at me. 'Meet my smiley shoe. Gotta put your best foot forward, ya?'

We link fingers as we walk into our park. The sky is blue and the grass is green and all that – and suddenly everything freezes.

On one of the benches, three women sit chatting. Three women I've known all my life. My mother and my two aunts. I know why they're here. It's because they know we hang out here. I'd told Maa everything yesterday, remember?

I want to rewind it all, to turn and run out again. Tia looks at my frightened face and says, 'Wassup? Seen a ghost?'

I nod my head at the bench. 'My mom and my aunts. Tia, they're probably here to meet you.'

'Did you know about it? Did you plan this?' she asks. I shake my head silently. She says after a beat, 'Are you okay with this?'

I look at this fantastic girl and I know then that I am. I'm not going to turn and run out with Tia. We're going to meet them together.

'Sharad?' she asks again.

'Relax! Just be your own sweet self. Everyone's gonna love you.'

'But I'm not sweet.'

My mother and my aunts have spotted us and are waving. The evening sun settles a warm golden tint over this scene that belongs in a photograph, to be framed in gold and hung on the wall.

'Come on,' I whisper. 'Meet the family.'

ALISHA

Someone's shaking me awake. Why? I want to sleep. Let me sleep. There's nothing to wake up for. A face comes into focus against the glaring sun. Ruhi. Go away, I want to sleep. Why is she rattling my shoulder? I try to lash out, but my arms don't move, I've got no strength left.

'You fell, Alisha,' Ruhi is telling me. Genius! 'Lucky you fell on this side of the wall, on to the terrace. It saved you, Alisha,' Ruhi gasps, catches her breath, like she's been running to get here. 'You could have fallen over the wall and...down there below.' She waves vaguely at nothingness, then opens her bottle and splashes water at me.

She holds the bottle to my lips and I choke on the water pooling into my mouth. And then I drink. In gulps. Thirsty.

Ruhi crouches, so we're both sitting up, backs propped up against the terrace wall. We sit there without saying anything. I swallow a few more mouthfuls of water quickly.

And then she starts talking. 'You're my hero, Alisha. I want to be you. I've always wanted to be you. No one messes with you. You're, like – strong, stunning. Help me.'

I steal a glance at her to see if she's being sarcastic. Me, fallen on the floor, broken, burnt.

She's not even looking at me. She carries on, her words tumbling out. She's trapped. Abusive relationship. Or not even a relationship. Predator. Older man. Says he's in college. She doubts it now. Could be working. In the porn industry? 'Is he?' she asks at one point but doesn't wait for my answer before continuing. Her parents don't know. No one knows. It would kill them. He's texting her. Pressurizing her to meet him. To pose for him. 'For sleazy pics,' she says. He already has a picture of her, he claims. Blackmail picture. From that party at Aman's. She'd blanked out, she says. She sounds terrified at the thought of what she might have done then. And going forward – should she just agree? Give in to his demands? Just this once? Get it over with? And then move on. What should she do?

I don't know what to say. But I must. I'm strong. She sees me as Wonder Woman. I can help, she knows that.

I turn to her and tell her, 'The first thing you do is go to a doctor, Ruhi. Get a check-up done. Even if you're not sure, it's playing on your mind. The doc can get tests done – pregnancy tests, STD tests, all that. To cross them off, Ruhi, don't worry. Be safe, first. Next, you go and report this pervert. Nothing he's done so far is okay. You know that, right? And you cannot, like, let it go.'

I've just survived a fall, I've just got my life back. And somehow, all that rises to the surface of my addled brain now is to get Ruhi to be safe. I mean, I sort of asked for this disaster flick I'm in. She didn't.

'I'll come with you if you want,' I tell her. 'Both to the hospital and to the police.'

Ruhi thinks it over a bit, then takes back her empty water bottle. 'Yeah, maybe. But I'll go alone. I can do it. I just need to plan it out. I can't disappear from home on the weekend, or my folks will get hyper. I'll make a doc appointment for next week. Thanks, Alisha.' She looks again at me and tilts her head. The mist in her eyes has cleared. 'And what's up with you? Why are you here? Jumping off walls? Fainting?'

I could tell her. Everything. It would lift that weight that suffocates me. All the time. Tell her, Alisha. Spill it. But of course, you won't. You're strong. You won't admit you need help, will you? I shrug. 'Chill, Ruhi! It's nothing. Nothing important.' Family mantra, remember?

Ruhi stands up and holds out a hand. I wave it away and lift myself off the floor. I've bruised the side of my leg when I fainted and toppled over. It's scraped, raw and bloody. I wince. Then I compose my face, and we walk to the stairs.

SHARAD

'Tia,' I say when we get to the bench, by way of introduction. Of course, this is all sudden and unexpected. I'm not prepared (hah, for a guy who revises every chapter four times over). But hey, I'm insanely proud. Happy. On cloud nine times nine times nine…

There are smiles all around.

They nod in greeting. 'Hello, dear,' says my eldest aunt, Badi Maa, Big Momma as her gangsta name would be. Not that I'd ever be caught calling her that. My mother reaches out her hand to me, which means I've got to unlink my fingers from Tia's and walk over to Maa. She squeezes my hand lovingly. I grin, embarrassed.

Tia and I stand. There isn't enough space on that bench for all five of us.

'Oh, nowhere to sit, dear,' my other aunt tells Tia, reading my mind. 'And you must be so exhausted, poor thing. You work as a waitress, Sharad says. It sounds like a tiring job, hard physical work.'

Tia smiles.

My aunt tuts. 'No child should ever have to work.'

Tia looks at me, a question in her eyes.

My older aunt is speaking again. 'And while you work, what does your father do? Works as…?'

'Badi Maa!' I stutter. This is turning into an inquisition. My face burns.

'My mother is a doctor,' Tia says.

'Very good, dear. Your mother works too. Like you. In our family, the women don't…hmm…*need* to work outside. We are the nurturers, we bind the family together – that's very important, no? We let the men take care of the money-making. Like Sharad will, some day.'

Tia's face is red. She's looking at her white sports shoes, at the pink smiley on one. I know she'll say something at any point now. I want to say something first to fend off this ridiculous barrage. I want to put my arm around her shoulder. My girl.

I don't, of course. It's not how things are done. In. Our. Family.

'Ria,' My older aunt says again.

'Tia. Maa, I told you,' I turn to my silent mother.

'Tia,' my aunt continues. 'Sorry. What kind of name is that?'

'A nice name.' Tia tries a smile.

'Yes, but from which place, dear?'

'My mother's from Assam. My dad was from here, Karnataka. It's just a name they liked. My mom has worked to raise three kids after my dad died. I work to help give my brother and sister some of the nicer things in life they deserve, like skates or birthday parties. Yes, it's tiring.'

In the silence that follows, my aunt says, 'And it would be nice for you to just sit back, to have someone take care of you, no? A nice boy from a nice family. So you have no money problems…?' She smiles, but I want to cancel, delete, undo, Ctrl-Z. This can't be happening. It is. And she's carrying on. 'We understand, dear. We understand you. We know what you're looking for.'

'No. You don't know me.' Tia takes a step back. She doesn't look at me. I turn to my mother. Frantic. Desperate. 'Maa!' I plead, 'Say something.'

My mother breaks her silence at last. 'Tia,' she says, 'Sharad is studying very hard to get into a top college. Nothing must disturb him. No one. You should focus on your studies too. Your mother will be proud of you then.'

Tia looks at me. I have so much I want to say. It's bubbling inside. Steaming. Frothing. But the words are stuck.

So much I want to say and I can't.[27]

Tia says instead, 'I understand. Sharad, don't try to reach out to me again.'

'Tia!' I manage at last. A squawk, really. But she's walking away. Dignified. Back straight. Her curls bobbing furiously all over.

18

ALISHA

I have to get away. I've tried to plod on. In zombie mode. I can't. I'm suffocating here. Got home after my spectacular fall on Friday evening to an intolerable weekend, every minute ticking by a mockery. And today, the start of a new week. Of nothing.

I have to run away. Away. Far. Away. Help. Who will help you, Alisha? Not AK. He hasn't even landed up in school. Not Sharad. He's got other priorities now. Not your parents. Not even food. Do you love food, Alisha, or hate it? Do you love yourself? Or…? Run, Alisha, run. Just run. You will get somewhere. Don't stand still. You will get nowhere. Run. Why? Why are you afraid? Of what? Who is chasing you? Run from yourself, Alisha. Outrun yourself. Run out of your skin. Become. Someone else.

I sat through class all of today. Mundane Monday. Munday, Mud-day! And then something snapped when the last bell rang. And I began to walk. With nowhere in mind. Just walk. On streets I've never seen. Into new, strange neighbourhoods. I've been out since after class. Six hours of walking, running, and getting nowhere. Of not going home. Phone on silent. I don't want to hear them call me. Ask me why I'm out so late. With disappointment in their voices. Because I'm so disobedient. Troublesome. Sullen. Hateful. Run, Alisha, from all the things they think you are. From all the names they call you. They don't really. But they think them in their heads. I break into a run again.

Legs burning. Soles on fire. Out of breath. Look at these streets. Look at people huddled in the cold under gunny sacks on the pavement. Am I luckier than them? Are they happier than me?

No street lights in this alley. I can sit here. Sleep. One night. Tomorrow, I'll think of what and where. It's so cold. I'm so tired. I'm hungry. There's food. Someone eating. A woman and her children. Three, and another at her breast. The older girl is feeding the younger ones. Such love. Like the pups. I can't tear my eyes away. They're eating rice. Plain rice. With a packet of sambar. One plastic packet secured with a rubber band. For four. No, five of them... There is a world out here that I've been sheltered from. Real problems. Huge burdens. Does that make mine lighter?

I sit unmoving, knees drawn up under my chin. While the street goes to sleep. The stores on the main road lower their shutters with clangs. Cats fight. Some men argue loudly. Tyres screech once in a while. A monologue from a drunk carries over on the slight breeze. Pavement dwellers pull their sheets, blankets, sacks over themselves. The woman and her children are holding one another, asleep already.

I look at shapes huddled down for the night. The sleep of the exhausted. This is the zone of the hard-working, Alisha. No time for self-pity, here, for questions, dilemmas, pretences…

I shut my eyes. Faces and voices crowd my brain – of my parents, classmates, Moni, AK, aunts, uncles. Disappointed shrugs. Worried eyes. I should call home. And say what? I'm out here somewhere on the streets, don't worry. Don't worry?

I should tell them I'm safe. But I'm not. I'm not at home here either.

You're not welcome anywhere, Alisha. You don't fit in. These people are not runaways like you, they are here because they have nowhere else to go. You do. And just like that, I know where I have to go. There's only one place I can feel safe.

I scramble to my feet and my bag falls over, spilling its contents. It's dark, but I hastily sweep whatever I can see back into the bag. I swing it over my shoulder and start walking again.

Quicker, Alisha, get away from here, get away to where you should be.

Quicker!

Run, Alisha, run.

AK

My dad's managed to give me what the car crash couldn't. A top-class fever. Since the news broke that egg-scrambling, mind-scrambling Thursday evening, I've been burning up. For the last four days, I've been tossing around, feverish – delirious, I'm told. Had to stay home from school. Even had to get the doc in. Nothing wrong with me. Physically, at least. Just happen to have a conscience, I guess. No clue from whom I've inherited that.

My dad's a criminal. My mom's an escapist. Neither cares how I feel about all this. Home was always just an illusion. Smoke and mirrors. Only showing us images of ourselves that we wanted to see.

I can't be part of this any more.

I'll just walk away. From the drama. From the wealth. Hah, like there's anything left. I'll go make my own home.

That used to be my dream with Alisha. She could have messaged. Just once. To ask me how I feel. She must have heard the news. They all must have. No one's called me. Too embarrassed? No one knows what to say to the black-hearted billionaire's son? I should take my cue and just exit scene here.

I'll call Alisha. I'll tell her I'm leaving. For good. She won't have to worry about me again. I'll be out of her life. Of this place. I'll go make my own life and I'll make it BIG. Bigger than my dad. Not that I have to compete with him. Or even think about him. Why did he do it, though? All those people and all their lifetime's savings... and he's lost it all – or run away with it? Where has he stashed it? Not that I want to know. Let him enjoy it. I hope it gives him more happiness than being with his family did.

Jaggu Kaka keeps bringing bread, soup, khichri into my room. The spaniels cuddle close. I can hear my mom pace in her room. Just a wall apart. But so far away.

I'll call Alisha. It's somewhere past midnight, isn't it? Who knows? I must talk to her now.

It's answered on the seventh ring. She's awake, she's answering it.

'Hey, Al,' I say.

'Wrong number.' A rough voice, a man's voice.

I look at the number. It's Alisha's. Strange. That didn't sound like anyone we know. It sounded slurred, drunk. Is Alisha in trouble? Has she lost her phone? Out at a party? Has she been kidnapped? No, this is not a movie.

I try calling her again. It rings out. And again. The eighth time I call, and let it ring out, is the last. The next time, the phone's switched off.

And then the shock gives way to panic. Alisha's phone isn't with her. She never, I mean ever, leaves it around. Where is she? She must be in trouble.

I have to find her. I have to get to her. I have to help her.

I take a set of car keys and rush down to where our cars are parked. In five minutes, I've gone from sick to pumped, foot pressed against the floor of the car, swerving my way across empty streets. Towards Alisha's house. She thinks I don't know where she lives. I followed her one day. I know. There's nothing I could not know about her.

I drive the car to a halt halfway across the pavement outside her housing society and vault over the gate, because I know her security guard is a deep sleeper. I run up to the fifth floor's narrow landing and lean on her doorbell. A whole minute passes before the door swings open. In the dim light inside, I see her dad in his white kurta-pyjama, his face ashen.

'Alisha?' I stutter.

'Where is she? She hasn't come home yet.' He sounds hysterical already. I doubt they have slept. Join the club. I'll fit right into this sleepless family. 'What has happened to her?'

'I don't know.'

'She didn't come home from school. We called everyone, no one knows. We went to the police, but they said youngsters often disappear like this. To wait until morning. She must be at a friend's house. Is she?'

'I don't know,' I repeat blankly.

Alisha's mom pushes her way to the front. 'Wait, I know who you are. You are that boy she is with all the time. I've heard her talk to Monisha. Where is she?'

And then I see the rage erupt in her dad's pale face. He reaches out with bony hands, grabs my collar and shakes it. 'Where is our girl?'

'I'm sorry, I don't know,' I stammer. I try to step back, extricate myself from his grip.

'You are that rich boy,' her dad yells. 'Your father is in the papers, thief, cheating hundreds of innocent people. You people think you can get away with anything? Where is my daughter?' He balls his fist and punches me. I try to shield my fractured arm; although I dodge, I take the brunt of the blow on my jaw. For a thin man, he packs a mean punch. Fuelled by his rage, I guess. And weakened by days of fever, I give in to the dizziness. I arch backwards, and then feel myself spiralling through air, down the flight of stairs.

ALISHA

Run, Alisha, to the one place you'll be safe.

Legs cramping, bag knocking against my back, I run. So dizzy. Out of breath.

Run. You've got to get there, Alisha. You know why. You'll be safe. You'll escape. Forever.

The school gate is locked. Of course. I run to the back where every kid knows the wall's broken. Jump over the gap. And in. Run. My heart fluttering against my ribcage, like a bird waiting to be set free. I run. To the building I know so well. To my usual spot. Wait. I'm coming. Home. The terrace. The wall. I'll be safe. I'll be free.

19

SHARAD

I've called her a hundred times over the weekend, and another hundred today. I've sent her more messages than I've written to everyone I've known in all my life combined. Granted, they say the same thing over and over again. But you think she'd reply to *one* of them? No. I type the same words. Over and over again. I should use my comp science skills and write a code to repeat in sequence every five minutes.

Tia?

I'm sorry

Please reply

Tia?

I can't live without you

I'm not being filmi

I'm sorry

We need to talk

I am going to do something dangerous

Stop me

Only you can stop me

Call me. Just 1 call
OK, 1 word
OK, 1 emoji
Counting till 10 till you call me
OK, here goes. 1 2 3 4
Tia?
Call me
Please please please please please please
Counting till 25
100
Please
I'm sorry
I'm chicken. I'm sorry that I'm chicken
Let me tell you why I'm so chicken
Fine, don't call
I'm leaving forever
You will be rid of me forever
Call once and then never again
Please
Tia?

AK

Again. I'm in hospital *again*. Making a habit of it. If anyone ever writes up this story, I'm going to be the guy in bed. I barely made it out of my sickbed at home and I'm back in one at the hospital.

My arm is in agony. While trying to shield it from Alisha's mad dad, I stepped back and fell down the stairs and had to be wheeled again into the X-ray room to find out how many more bones I've broken. Somehow the pain seems worth it. Something to take my mind off things. I've been fitted with an ortho collar, the kind that you see grandpas wearing in parks. And they're bandaging the cuts and scrapes from my fall. I don't tell them it's because of a blow from Alisha's mad dad.

And then he appears. The mad dad himself. Like a bad dream. Except I'm not dreaming. He's the guy who drove me here. After I had my epic fall, the family came rushing over and suddenly I went from villain to victim. 'Are you hurt?' 'Can you open your eyes?' 'Can you stand?' And then, when I tried to lever myself up, I let loose an agonized yell as excruciating pain shot from my neck downwards. My entire left side felt like a truck was repeatedly driving over it. To my embarrassment, Alisha's short, thin dad had to support my six-foot, muscled bulk down to his car. More screaming, cursing from me. (Please don't judge me, I don't usually use this language, I told them.) And they got me here. All three of them. The mad dad, mom and Al's sis, Monisha. Happy family scene at the hospital. Just not my family.

Remembering my family sends fresh pain coursing through every inch of my body, even the bits not broken. I can cry, they'll just peg it down to my broken bones.

Big boys don't cry, remember?[28]

Alisha's dad has been talking to the doctor in the Accident and Emergency ward, and he now moves aside the blue curtain and sits down on the plastic chair at my bedside. Monisha and her mom are on a bench outside, I'm told. Only one attendant at a time is allowed in here.

Déjà vu. Sharad, my unlikely saviour, sitting there. Now, an even more unlikely one.

He's a quiet man, Alisha's dad. When he's not being mad, that is. He sits silently while I count the curtain rings and then he says, 'What justice is there in this world?'

It seems like a question I should know the correct answer to. 'None?' I venture.

'None is right. I've done nothing wrong. We are decent people, God-fearing, pious people, we feed the poor, we save for our girls' future. And what good has come of it?'

'None?' I say, more confident now.

'None is right. Look how Alisha has turned out. Turned her back on us. Gone wild. She has hurt us in front of our family. Time and again. And now she's run away. We love her. She hates us in return.'

I don't answer. I'm not getting into this family drama, oh no. I've got enough of mine to run a Netflix miniseries.

He carries on. 'We have only ever loved her. And she has brought us only pain. Each time, a fresh insult, another slap in the face. It's like she's looking for new ways to punish us, but we don't know what for.'

I stay silent.

'You know her well. Better than us, maybe. Tell me, why does she hate us so much?'

I shrug. Ow! That hurt. I stay silent.

'Are we bad parents? Or has she fallen into bad company? Something must be wrong.'

I find myself speaking. 'It's not about bad. She's confused. She wants to be someone you wouldn't approve of. At least, that's what she thinks. She doesn't hate you. At all. She's never once said that. She feels that you don't understand her. So maybe she's not exactly like the rest of your family. She wants to be a star. And you want her to be normal, ordinary. But she's not. She's extraordinary. Intelligent. Sensitive. Talented. Special. She's special.'

He looks at me. I expect he's going to say that I'm young and foolish, what would I know of life.

He says, 'I didn't give you enough credit. You seemed like just another spoilt rich kid. But you're not bad.'

I'm deeply launched into my spiel now. Maybe I have a future as a lawyer, counsellor, sales guy. Got it – a politician! 'When she returns, give her a chance. Let her be the way she wants to be. Support her. Talk to her. Listen to her. See the view from her side of the universe. Just be there for her. It's what we need from our folks, even though we don't ask.'

He knows I'm not talking only about Alisha now. He nods. '*Beta*, your parents love you too. No matter what they are, what they do. We parents, you know, we don't have a formula. We don't know sometimes how to show our love. You know? We make mistakes. We're human too.'

I choke up suddenly. I look down.

The curtain parts again. Monisha walks in, followed by a nurse who says sternly, 'Only one attendant. One.'

Alisha's dad places his hand on my head. For a few seconds. His blessing. From a father. Even if it's not mine. Then he goes out and Monisha hands me my phone. She looks over her shoulder to see that he has left and whispers, 'I saw you called Didi. What did she say?'

'I didn't –' I begin.

'Please. Please tell me where she is. I won't tell them.' She nods her head towards the exit door. 'I must know. I can't stand it – with her being out there somewhere, without knowing.'

I look at her thirteen-year-old face, crumpled, lips trembling, and I tell her, 'She said she'll be back home soon.'

I'm a liar. Son of a thief.

ALISHA

The door to the terrace is locked. They must lock it at night. I'm trapped. No help.

I need a light to check the lock.

I rummage in my bag for my phone. I can't find it in the pocket. Frantic, I shake out the contents of my bag. The books tumble out. An old rose from AK, dried and flattened between the pages of my diary. Pens. Ruler. Stickers. Earphones. Comb. Bottle. Tissues. Beads. Skull pendant. Project file. Black lipstick. No. It's gone. Fallen out when my bag turned over in the alley. Nooo!

I kick the door. Throw my weight against it. I hammer at it till my head spins. Till I slump to the floor. I can't escape. Not even here.

AK

Twenty-seven missed calls for me? I scroll through the phone Monisha's handed me and see twenty-seven missed calls from the home line. Either there's been another roaring emergency. Or someone's noticed I'm gone. I press the call-return button.

It's early morning now. Still dark outside. My favourite time, of late, to navigate the highs and lows of my life – and the Bangalore streets, of course, ha!

Jaggu Kaka answers it. 'Baba!' He breaks into sobs. He's been calling me, he says. He was afraid of where I'd gone and what I'd do. He doesn't think I should be roaming around when I'm ill. 'Come home,' he tells me finally. 'It will all be okay.'

I'm crying too. Someone does care. Of course, he does. Someone very, very important to me. Someone who's carried me through every childhood fall, chipped tooth and broken bone. The voice on the phone changes. He's handed it to my sister. Neo barks, 'And, just where are you?'

'In the hospital,' I say.

She takes the details and rings off with, 'I'll be there in a jiff if you've left any cars un-smashed up, that is, for me to drive. I'll bring you home. Dumbass!'

Neo Unplugged. I have to smile.

I press the staff call bell, and the very efficient nurse, who's been on her feet all through her night shift, appears at once. 'What's wrong? Are you in pain?'

'No, I'm fine.' I mean it. I'm wanted at home. Loved. Missed. Needed. What pain could I possibly crib about?

I tell the nurse that my sister is on her way and to tell Alisha's parents who are waiting outside to go home. I'll be okay.

And then I wonder how *they* will ever be okay again. Without Alisha.

Where is she?

SHARAD

Late nights aren't my thing. Weren't. Unless I was at my books, Maa hovering around like a giant moth. With mugs of hot milk. Tonight, I'm back home to curious looks. Dinner happened without me. I'm back even later than my cousins, who shut shop at ten most nights. No one says anything. I've said nothing.

Not since the Tia incident.

Three days of silence. No speaking to Tia, my family, my classmates, not even to those wise-mouths who look mournfully at me from my wall.

So Maa doesn't ask me why I am so late tonight. And I don't tell her.

That after school I went to the café. That I sat outside near the suspicious phone-cover seller. And peered in through the window. Where people ordered sandwiches. And laughed like they meant it. And flirted. And drank coffee. And coughed up water when they laughed too hard. And took phone calls. And spoke more on their phones than to each other. And got bills. And swiped cards. And waved to Tia when they left. Where Tia worked and talked to everyone except me. Where Tia didn't look out of the window though it's so large. Where Tia didn't want to see me.

Where I realized I was invisible once again.

When the only light I ever saw at the end of the tunnel, turned off.[29]

That's what happened tonight, and I won't tell Maa even if she asks me. But she doesn't.

I sit at my desk and open my books. I no longer know what to look forward to. I see only a blank white wall in front of me.

20

RUHI

The hospital looks peaceful at seven in the morning. White-uniformed staff changing shifts. The ones going out joking and the ones coming into work, serious. A few trolleys with breakfast stuff roll by. Early morning visitors, well-muffled, carry baskets of home-cooked food for their families. The anonymity is reassuring. No one knows me here.

'Ruhi?' And I've barely got in through the main door. So much for anonymous silence. Alisha's family is leaving, and her mother comes over to hold my hands. '*Beta*, do you know where Alisha is? We are worried about her.' I shake my head. No. She goes on, 'Please, *beta*, ask your friends. Tell her to come home. We are so frantic.' She wipes her eyes with her pallu and says, 'Look how inconsiderate I am. Why are you here, *beta*? And all alone? You're sick?'

'No, no, I'm – um – here to visit a friend.' How glibly I lie, once-upon-a-time-good-girl Ruhi.

And to my surprise, she points at the Emergency ward. 'Of course. He's in there.'

Dumbly, I walk in through the door with its 'Do Not Enter' sign. What do you do in an emergency then? Die outside? I enter.

'Ruhi?' I turn to the furthest bed in the room and see an equally surprised AK lying there, bandaged, waving. What is this – a school reunion?

As I mentioned, I've barely exchanged any words with AK through the many years we've been classmates. Different orbits. So now, this is Awk-ward! 'Hey, all well?' I start stupidly, because quite obviously he is in the Emergency ward of a hospital with his neck in a brace and arm in a sling. Not the scientific definition of 'all well' for sure.

'Seen Alisha?' he asks.

'No. Her folks asked me outside. You know what's happened?'

'She's vanished. Her dad threw me down the stairs.'

I giggle. I can't help it. Whatever hellhole I'm in, the image of Alisha's very puny father throwing the Hulk down the stairs is funny!

He breaks into a wide grin too. 'I know. So why are you here? Class planning a party for me?'

He's not bad. I have forty-five minutes to kill before my appointment, so I sit on the plastic chair by his bed and to my surprise, we slip into an easy chat. I tell him how my parents think I'm going out this early in the morning, before class begins, for 'joint-study' with a friend.

'You can "joint-study" my joints. Want to see what's broken where?' He points to the X-rays clipped to the bed's metal frame. And I chuckle some more. But then as I talk, I go from giggles to tears.

I start with the party and the cokes that were not cokes, and the handsome guy who took me to find Alisha, except I was high and passed out, and he took pics of me that he is using to blackmail me. I showed AK some of the messages on my phone.

'This dude needs to be thrashed, Ruhi. This is so not okay.'

'Yeah, sure,' I roll my eyes at his splints. 'You gonna thrash him?'

I tell AK how I'm here for the earliest appointment I could book before rushing off to school. A Tuesday 8 a.m. slot with the gynaecologist. Twilight had, upon my persistent hassling, finally assured me that nothing 'like that' (he said) had really happened that night. I was so out of it and kept barfing apparently. He claims his friends were totally turned off. Thank you, God! But he's keen to 'take it on from here'. I show AK the message which says:

> Let's get wild, baby, you'll see how much fun it is. We'll keep the cameras on so you can see it later

I'm crying by then. That always gets me bawling. I feel stupid. Trapped. Helpless.

I don't know how to get myself out of this whirlpool.[30]

AK lets me sob it all out. He keeps patting my hand like I'm his dog. Nicer than it sounds because he's always sharing pics of his dogs, he adores them. I tell him that I'm going to ask the gynae about my options. Because one thing's for sure. I can't let my parents see the blackmail pic Twilight's threatening to send them. It would kill them. My cutting my hair gave them palpitations… imagine the after-party pic.

'Ruhi, and what about those pics or vids he takes next? Listen to yourself. You're such a brainiac, you can't believe anything he says. He's going to blackmail you again and again. You can't do anything with this dude. Stop it. Now. Your parents will understand. Tell them.' AK is leaning towards me earnestly. 'No way are you going to meet him again. Or have anything to do with him. Got it? We'll go to the cops. We'll put him behind bars. I'll help you. We'll all help you. What are friends for?' I break into even louder sobs till a nurse comes over angrily. 'Go out. You're disturbing the other patients.'

AK hands me tissues and I grab a few before running off for my appointment. I'm feeling loads lighter. *We*, he said. I'm part of a *We* again. It's only much later that I realize I hadn't asked him how he feels about his dad being splashed all over the papers. Not a very helpful segment of the We, am I?

AK

I should break his bones! In fact, broken bones make for great self-awareness. Look at my time in this hospital.

It's where I've had the conversations that have made the most sense. Sharad, Alisha's dad, Alisha's sis and now Ruhi. What's happening to her makes me boil. #@$$$##! I may have said some of that aloud because the nurse throws me a disgusted look.

And then Neo is here. My loving, caring older sister.

'I want to smack you so hard. Maybe the few bits of your body that are still connected will crack too. Why are you on this self-destructive spree?' She looks furious and not so loving and caring at all. 'Like, haven't we got enough to worry about otherwise? Without you slamming into trees and sliding down staircases?'

'All accidents. Really, Neo.'

She plonks on the side of the bed, bouncing me up. I wince. I suspect she did that on purpose. She's in her sweatshirt and shorts, her hair in a sweatband. 'I hope this doesn't take too much time. Gotta make it for my run before the sun scorches my skin off. Max and I have this online competition going – who clocks more kilometres. So, hurry. Told the nurse to get your discharge papers ready.'

She sounds like my dad, barking orders and getting people to hop to it.

'I'm deeply sorry my broken bones are taking you away from your run or boyfriend or whatever.'

'Them bones are fixed now. Stop whining! The neck's just a bit of a sprain. Back bruised. And the arm is healing. Sorry to plug your self-pity binge.'

'Oh, then I might as well spring off to school today,' I say sarcastically.

'Yep, don't you dare dream of pulling another sickie. If you're well enough to whizz around town, you're well enough to go to school and face the music. What Dad did has nothing to do with you. You go do your thing, your day, whatever.'

She's read my mind. I've been wondering how long I can stay home using the injury card. But the real reason is because I don't want to be the son of 'that man in the papers'. I've already bunked two days. I don't want to face the questions, the sniggers, the loaded looks, the whispers behind my back, the comparisons, the anger or the pity.

But I'll go. I'm gonna man up and go.

While waiting for the papers to arrive, Neo tells me the police happened late last night. The first of their visits. A 'surprise' check of Dad's room and the rest of our house. 'Like we'd got secret tunnels leading to the bundles of money he stashed away. A hidden trapdoor in our apartment floor to the house below. So nice if you lived below us to have bundles of cash drop into your slowly simmering dal makhani, yeah?'

They questioned her, she said, and also our mom and Jaggu Kaka. Seriously? I erupt: 'What's he got to do with it? Like his threadbare sweater is threaded with gold. Didn't they check the spaniels? Maybe their little doggie baskets are lined with cash. Hey, Neo, seriously, maybe – like? Did you check? We could still be rich.' She bites back a smile.

We're both decently mad at each other. She, because I interrupted her precious daily two-hour run and workout. And me, because she's mad at that.

She says, 'Anyway, Dad's probably on his way to a beach in a false beard and red wig. His money would already be in offshore accounts all over. No way will we ever know. Some day maybe you'll get a call from some sunny island and go join him on his yacht.'

'How's Mom taking it?'

'A lot of sleeping pills, that's what she's taking. The doc's got her on a hefty dose. She's been, you know, wasted most of yesterday.' Neo looks searchingly at me, then says, 'Hey, dumbass. Don't worry about her, okay? She's made tough. She's gotten through worse. She will rebound. Unlike you. You're a softie.'

I'm outraged. 'I'm not…' I splutter. 'I'm gonna bounce back – and how! I'll make it big. You wait and see. I mean, I'll make it big in a straight way, not underhand. I mean…'

'Yeah, yeah. Let's just see you make it out of this bed on your own for now.'

I ask her again, 'Neo, seriously though. Didn't he leave us any money? We're his family.'

'Of course, he did, duh! Fat lot of good it will do. Most of it will go into repaying his debts.'

I say and I mean this, 'I'll work, Neo. I'll pay it all back. Every bit. I don't want those people to suffer.'

'Good! Maybe you can be a stuntman? At least they'll pay you to break your bones.'

Just when I'm getting all emo, she has to spoil it all.

The papers arrive and she goes off to sign them and stuff, and then we're on our way home. 'Get ready super-fast and I'll drive you to school. They'll understand the situation… I don't want to see your hangdog look around the house all day. And if anyone in school asks about Dad, tell them to ask me. If anyone messes with you, they get a dental reconstruction – for free. Why do you think I've been lifting weights for years?' She flexes a bicep and winks at me. I laugh.

21

SHARAD

Hit the C. A new record. For me. Grade C aggregate. Dropped from a steady A+ to a C. Well done, me!

But it was bound to happen. Tanking in my exams. I am not the supercomputer everyone thinks I am. I just study harder. I want it more, so I work towards it more. I need success. I need it to get me out of here. And yet I'm now home with my C and it's not going to get me out of anywhere, any time soon.

Maa goes in and out of the room, like a chill wind. She shoots me looks, which I notice thanks to my well-developed peripheral vision. But I don't turn. Let her suffer. Like me. Let the world suffer. I've done nothing wrong, so why me? Why me and Tia? Why us? But there isn't an us. And there won't be an us because of them. Because of her. Maa.

It's not even dawn and I've checked my online marksheet, like I always do. The school uploads it overnight. And I'm probably the only enthu one who checks it this early.

'Marks were due today?' Maa asks finally. 'Show me?'

I turn my laptop towards her and see the screen light up her eager face. I watch as the hope in her eyes fades into nothingness. I see her upturned lips straighten out, her brow crinkle. She backs away like the marks have scalded her. She retreats to her prayers. They will protect her. They will come through for her. Something will happen. My mother has unshakeable faith. Nothing I do, not even getting the kind of marks she sees as a deliberate breach of her trust in me, can destroy her. She has weathered worse. And her prayers have pulled her through. Her lips moving, she turns her back on me. And withdraws into her own world, where no betrayals, girlfriends or grades can enter. She sits on the edge of the bed and sways.

I love to see her like that. Usually. It makes me feel safe too. She has, all my life, blown a bubble of prayer around me. So that nothing will harm me, because she strongly believes that nothing will, and it has always made me feel invincible.

And then, I want to burst that bubble. I want to be cruel. I want to hurt her the way she hurt me.

This is not me. I'm not like this. But this too is me. Some part of me.

'Maa?' I say. She keeps rocking, murmuring, eyes closed.

'Listen,' I say. She doesn't hear me.

I know the word to burst the bubble, though. Sharp enough to slice through it. And I use it.

'Tia,' I say.

She stops. Stops her whispering.

'I love you. But I also like Tia.' She tries to carry on, tries to rock again, but I know I've got her attention. Her lips don't move.

'You let me down. You hurt me and Tia that day. Why did you? Why did you betray my trust, Maa?'

She doesn't raise her voice. Maa never does. She says, 'I? *I* let *you* down? See your marks, Sharad. *You* let me down. All my hopes. You are the one thing that keeps me alive. And don't pretend you don't know that. Everything I ever did was for you. I stayed silent in this house for years and years, and outside it, among friends and relatives and parties – because I know that you would one day prove them all wrong. That you would silence their wagging tongues. That the boy with no father would one day shine brighter than all of them and their children. That you are destined for a path of greatness, the brightest star, the envy of every peer and mother. That you would get a wonderful job and house and marry a wonderful girl so that I could look after my wonderful grandchildren. That we would be so happy, it would be everyone else's dream to be like us. You were my one hope. And you let me down.' She hasn't looked at me once. She hasn't raised her voice at all. She speaks from a place of love. And hurt.

'But Tia isn't about you. This is about me. Tia makes me happy. This is my life, Maa.'

'What do you know about life? Happiness is getting out of this place, you said, Sharad, and with an A plus, you could buy yourself any life you wanted. That girl has taken away your A plus.'

'Which girl?'

Maa stops.

'Her name, Maa. Say it. She's not "That Girl". She's Tia. And I'm going to give her a chance. Hah, or more like ask her to give me a chance.'

'Sharad, stop acting so filmi. You're just a child. This love-shove won't get you into the college of your choice. There are those children who work hard, and those who daydream and fool around. The two cannot be one and the same. I have nothing against that girl...'

'Tia,' I interrupt.

'All youngsters have crushes; you think you are in love, but that dies out. And then what are you left with?' She looks at me then. 'You think you're the only one who ever rebelled against their family to fall in love? And what did that get me?' Me, she said, referring to herself. Not you, Sharad. Me.

She's not playing fair. My father disappeared on her. It doesn't mean it has to happen again. It's not a formula.

My mother lifts herself off the edge of the bed and walks to the door. 'I'll get you your energy drink now. Before you get ready for school.'

If you meet my mother, you'd think she's sweet, that's true. And soft. Her arms twig-thin and blue-veined, stray greys plaited into her long hair, her face grave and her shoulders hunched. But she isn't soft. She's made of steel. I've always been insanely proud of her because of it. And never had it turned against me. Not until now.

She's strong and dignified and loving. And I don't have it in me to knock that down. But I stand firm, at least I think I do. 'Maa, I'm going to do both. If I crack my grades, will you believe that my success has nothing to do with Tia or you or my father or the lack of one or anyone else's father or – well, anyone else – just me?'

She walks out, with a thin smile in my direction. No yes. No no. A smile. Wait, it says, this was just Round One.

AK

Home is like a circus. It often is now. Since the news broke, it's been crazy. All sorts of people descended on us, with gloomy faces, shrugs, nods – like they were paying us a condolence visit, like we needed to offer them an explanation, like they'd been part of our hive.

I walk home, straight into the melee even this early in the morning. Neighbours, including a few whom I've never seen before and I assume are merely claiming front-row seats at the drama, are crawling around our living room, sipping from cups that Jaggu Kaka keeps bringing out on a tray. Someone has ordered samosas. Really? Picnic at the scene of crime? I recognize a couple of folks from my father's long-since-separated extended family, in his room, sitting on his bed and nodding grimly at each other in a series of told-you-so's. Another group sits around my mother at the dining table, asking syrupy questions about how she is holding up. Holding up what? The chandelier? She's her usual contained self, straight as a statue, chin up, hair perfectly caught up in her bun, knot – what's it called – whatnot, what knot, hah! Maybe I'm getting hysterical, this is all so unreal. I almost want to go back to the hospital; it made more sense. There are even a few policemen who are asking random people random questions. And the media questioning the police. Everyone wants to know how no one knew anything until now.

Neo has just entered the house. She was parking the car while I came up to get ready for school. And she totally loses it. I guess days of being in the unwelcome glare has gotten to her too.

'What the eff is going on here? Out, all of you! This is our home. Out! Does the doormat say "Welcome All to Trample All over Our Home"? No! Do we look like we're dying to tell you what we don't even know? No! Does the carpet hide a map to the hidden millions?'

Shhh, Jaggu Kaka tries to pat Neo's arm. But she's on a roll. She stands, holding our main door open and yelling at everyone until they begin to file out. Sullen. Sheepish. Reluctant. But out. Only the policemen stay on until Neo announces, 'From now on, only our lawyer will talk to you.'

What lawyer? How does Neo know all this? I stand stupefied. Respect! I am so in awe of this sister whose kickassness I had no idea about until now.

My new role model. No, wait! I've just about dislodged Dad from that pedestal. No one goes up there now. I've got to give up on this whole hero-worship thing.

Time to find out what I'm made of. Not Dad, not Neo. Me. Time to head to school.

RUHI

Got to school while the assembly bell was clanging away. My mind's ringing too. So much. So much to process. Only a few days ago, I had no worries except whether I'd get an A or an A plus. Least of my worries now.

The first person I notice is AK. Had he flown out of hospital this fast? After calling in sick since Thursday, he's actually made it here. Wow! Ultra-brave of him because he's got to look at all these kids in the eye, and they all know what a dirtbag his dad has turned out to be. And he's high-fiving and punching guys like it's all okay. Must take guts. Good for him. I can see some kids whispering and giving him the eye-roll. Fly over them all, AK. He catches me looking at him and grins.

He's stepped out of a sleek car, as usual. Don't ask me about cars, don't know one from the other. His sister, Niharika, has dropped him off, I think. She's epic. If I wasn't crushing on Alisha, I'd probably be crushing on her.

Alisha!

And then it all adds up like the math sums I'm so good at. Because I'm the only one in the universe who knows where she is.

I go up to AK and his gang of thugs – Aman and all – you know. And I tug at his sleeve. And to the amazement of his gang, he slips out of that group and walks out with me. I'm feeling big and important and happening and smart and all that at once.

'What? Did something happen at the doc's?' AK whispers.

'Uh-oh. No. All good. Got a lecture that went on forever. Adults talk so much. I'll tell you later. This is about Alisha.'

22

ALISHA

The light's splintering my head. Somebody turn it off! I open my eyes and see it's daylight, slanting through a high, dusty window. I'm curled into a foetal position. Legs cramping. Stomach heaving. Lips dry. Mouth raw. Eyes crusted. I raise an arm to wipe my nose on my sleeve and bite back the pain. Every bit of me is on fire. Though it's cold. Stone-cold floor. On the landing outside the door. To the terrace. I remember now. I couldn't open the door. I couldn't get away.

Maybe I'll just lie here till I feel better. No one will find me here. There's a stack of old discarded desks and cardboard cartons piled up in the corner of the landing. I can just lie there. I want to sleep on and on. Oblivion. No one can ever see me like this. Like anyone would even care. Let them remember me as the North Star, dazzling and mysterious. Let them worship that Alisha. The one with the flashing eyes and black lipstick, the chains dancing across her chest, the bracelets and beads snaking over her arms. The Alisha every other girl wanted to be. Not this broken creature. Not this me. This is not me.

And then I hear the one thing that can make my nightmare even worse.

Footsteps. Running up the stairs. No! Past the fourth-floor landing. They're coming towards me. They're coming for me. No!

Nowhere to fly to. The door won't open. No one can see you like this, Alisha, you – the shining star, the spinning dervish, the goddess. No! Help me, save me, let them not see me. Please.

I crawl to the corner and push myself under one of the desks. A twisted wooden splinter pierces my thigh as I push myself in further into the dark. Into the muffled sounds, perhaps rats, cockroaches, spiders. I don't care. It's people I need to stay away from now.

I grab the largest cardboard carton and flatten it over me as I hunch in there. I draw my legs up under my chin and make myself small, silent.

'Alisha!'

Go away. Please. Help me and leave me alone. Go away! Don't find me like this. I can't take it. Please.

'Alisha, are you here?'

I shrink into the corner and the panic makes me heave again. I turn my head to the side and retch as silently as I can. But I've dislodged something. A rat runs out and someone screams.

Hands tugging at my cardboard cover. I hold on with raw fingers, look up with frightened eyes.

'Alisha!'

No! This can't be happening. I need to shut it all out. Leave me alone. Don't find me here like this. Alisha isn't here. This is not Alisha. Go away, all of you.

Silhouetted against the light, I see a group of them. My classmates. Haloed against the skylights. Six or seven, headed by Ruhi. Traitor! They've come to gloat over me at my weakest. To see me crushed. Sick. Puking. Frightened. Destroyed. They will now see me as I really am. And trash me for who I tried to be. Look how pathetic she is, they will tell each other. Eww, how she smells, they will turn their faces away. They will laugh at me.

No one's laughing.

Why not? I would if I saw me. If I saw Pompous Me, now punctured. Deflated.

Ruhi's saying, 'Thank God we found you, Alisha.'

Why? Why would they care about what happens to me? Get out! I'm screaming in my head.

Mihika is kneeling, she's got a bottle of water that she's opening for me. Rohan's leaning over, 'You okay?' Jonathan's trying to lift the table so I can crawl out. Someone's saying, 'Let me get your bag.' Someone else is holding me by my wrist, 'Let's go downstairs.'

Why do you care, you people? I've got no power over you any more, why do you still care?

A voice I know so well. No, not him too. He's saying, 'She's fine. She's great. Alisha's tough, you guys. Don't worry. She just had a bit of a toss, that's all. Must have blacked out.'

AK.

They're around me now, easing me out from under the table. And I'm letting myself be eased out. I'm drinking the water. Allowing my elbow to be held.

With the mask off, with the wings off, with the crown off...am I still worth liking?[31]

AK is holding out a hand. His other arm is in plaster up to his shoulder. His shirt too has some sort of wrapping around it and his neck looks like it's in a collar. Another accident? Is that why he hasn't been in school? He looks more bashed up than this smashed table. And *he* is trying to help *me* up? What a laugh!

Only, it's then that I begin to cry.

AK

Alisha is a star. She's dope. She is...what's that they say? Grace under fire? Or whatever. Once she's cleaned up and eaten something, and whoa, does she eat – she sits through the day at school. And aces it. No whining and running home. No blaming anyone for what's happened to her. I hope she tells me what's happened. I'm still here for her. If she wants me to be. A shoulder to cry on. Though both mine are currently out of order, thank you very much.

Even at her lowest, she's inspiring. She gives me the strength I need to face the day, the gossip-mongering, the below-the-belt hits by so-called friends. But then, I've got plenty of real friends too. The guys who slap my back – Ow, you guys, that hurt! 'Really?' asks Aman, and then does it again. Sharad says, 'How did you survive this time, without me?' Ha! Funny!

Neo picks me up after school and we drop Alisha home first. I am beginning to like these drives with my fierce sister. I don't think I've spoken to her as much in all the last few years combined. And I get the idea she likes this too. Or else why would she be driving me around? It's not like anyone can make her do anything she doesn't want to. Not unless they want their jaws dislocated for trying.

'So this babe's the special one, huh?' Neo asks after we've dropped Alisha off. I grin. She bites her lip and after a beat, says, 'You want to talk to the love of *my* life?'

This is big! She's never offered to let me talk to Max before. But this time, I've got something else I want to ask her.

'No, Neo, I want to talk to you.' I wonder how to start, then just come out with it. 'Neo, you knew? All those years, did you know, did you, like – suspect, at least, that things weren't on the level with Dad? Did you know that Mom knew?

'No rocket science. You knew too.' Direct. Honest. No pulling back her punches.

I guess I did know somewhere deep down – and didn't want to face it? I wanted us to be the perfect family. I guess I knew when Neo, who barely scraped through school, got into the college of her dreams in the US. A little offer of help from my dad, I'm guessing

– to help build their new robotics lab or something. Guessing, guessing, people! Hands-up emoji. I guess I knew long before that too. How roadblocks and hurdles magically disappeared when money was thrown at them. How we got the best tables at restaurants that were full, front-row seats at concerts that were sold out, complainants suddenly shutting up, critics turning sweet, police reports withdrawn because of a change of heart, my mother's screaming accusations that ended in a new car or a donation to her favourite charity. Things that were just this side of not-so-right. Nothing major or traceable ever. Just things that got smoothened out when my dad entered the scene. And which kept me awake at night for that extra half hour till I told myself it was just the way of the world and I would understand when I grew up. When I grew out of my conscience.

I glance at Neo at the exact moment she grins at me. Yeah, she gets me all right!

'You'll be okay, baby bro,' she says. 'You've got me. You lucky thing!'

RUHI

A shift. Gradual. As slow as hair growing back. As soft as the sun's rays sliding across my room. I'm not Baby any more. Made it clear to my parents. And will to Twilight. Not baby. And that's the other thing. Certain. I just feel so much more definite about things now. There's no flip-flop, roll-a-dice, maybe or maybe-not.

Sitting on the front bench in class this morning, I had turned slightly so that I could keep an eye on Alisha, at the back, as usual, leaning against the wall, long legs stretched out. Two rows away, AK sat awkwardly, shifting his weight from one side to the other with a grimace each time. It must hurt like crazy. Not just his scrapes and bruises. And that's the point. The courage. So brave. So, so brave. So so so! Showing up for class. No excuses. Being there when there was for sure going to be snarkiness or rumours or whatever. Being there. Showing up.

Brave.

Mumma breaks into my thoughts with the call to tea, and I go out and sit at the table. I'm going to be brave too and tell them everything. Right from the little black skirt onwards. And they will hold me tight like they always do. And I will go back into that familiar blanket of warmth, love, security.

Wait! Is there a 'going back'? Can I? More importantly, do I want to?

They look at me now, almost afraid. Like I'm a feral animal. Someone they don't recognize any more. The child whose every cry they shushed is now an enigma. Like I've sprouted a second nose. Papa doesn't even look me in the eye in case he sees something he doesn't want to. He busies himself with his tea, muttering in monosyllables. Mumma makes filler talk. The neighbour's in-laws are in town. There will be a bank strike on Tuesday. The water tanks are going to be cleaned on Thursday.

Looking at them does something to me. All that stuff about them closeting me, suffocating me – still true. But they did it because that's the only way they knew to be. I'm not a baby any more. I don't need them to protect me. But. But. But it strikes me out of nowhere. They're the ones who need protecting. Keep the world spinning the way it is. They're good people. They need to be treated right. It's no big deal. Just a gradual shift.

'I'm sorry,' I say as I nibble on the tip of a samosa. 'I'm sorry about the last few days. I've got to tell you guys something.'

Papa's eyes well up with tears at once. Mumma stops nattering.

'I was just stressed out because of studies.' I look at Papa's face while I say it. Without batting an eye. Good-girl Ruhi is telling a lie. But. But.

'Are you sure there's nothing else, Ba…Ruhi?' Mumma comes over to pull me into a hug. Into the softness of her belly. Let me back in there!

'Nothing else. No need to worry. My hair will grow back. I just – wanted to do something different.'

'It's okay, we understand.' Mumma melts at once. 'We just want you to be happy. Safe.'

Happy. Safe. What I'm not.

'I'm fine,' I say. 'It will all be fine.'

At some point, you stop blaming the world, and start doing something about it.[32]

And as I say that, I realize: I can't tell them. It will crush them. But I'm dead sure about what I have to do.

To make this all go away. I can't keep this waiting any longer. It's got to be now.

I tell Twilight that I will meet him at ten tonight. 'Somewhere quiet. Where there's no one around,' I say. 'Come to school. There's a break in the back wall and you can get in. The guard snoozes in his booth at the front gate. The grounds are deserted at night. We'll be alone.'

23

SHARAD

Round 2 – 3 – 4 – 400? I feel like I've been fighting this war ever since I was little. This time, backup's been called in.

I walk in from school to the clan gathered around the dining table. My uncles and cousins are back home early, so it must be a momentous occasion, right?

Badi Maa is the commander-in-chief. My uncles allow her to make most decisions. They usually get home so exhausted after their shops shut that they don't even bother turning on the geysers for a hot bath. She gets the help to switch them on ten minutes before they arrive. Just takes one flick of her finger at someone. One flick of a geyser switch in each bathroom.

'Sharad *beta*, come, sit and have a mithai,' she gestures to the chair beside her, lying dangerously empty. I go over. I sit. I pick up a sweet. Told you, we're all centrally controlled here. I have no will of my own.

'Now, what's all this I hear? You're angry with us?' She pats my back affectionately. And it makes me want to throw up.

'You are our baby, our youngest. How does that make us feel?'

I sit quietly. I know when questions aren't questions. I'll wait for them to build up to the real biggie, the climax.

Badi Maa continues, 'You made us feel upset, that's what you made us feel. When you misunderstood us about That Girl. She is not like us, *beta*.'

The barfi turns into barf. I choke, burp. Still not time. I look down, though now my eyes are smarting and I can feel my ears burn.

'Oh, come on, *beta*, you took it badly. That thing with That Girl. We have to take care of you. We are your mothers. You are such an innocent. You don't know what's bad for you.'

With her next words, she delivers the knockout punch. 'You don't want to be the one to break up this family, no? Look at us, look at her. Do you think we are the same? She's been brought up differently. And family matters, you know. She's very smart and all. Very nice girl, I'm sure, very nice, we all thought. But do you think she will fit in here? If you say so, then okay, we will reconsider. But you know how we are. We are humble, simple people. Look how close we are, we took in our sister and her son without a murmur when she was abandoned.'

I can't look at Maa. I want to scream. Break something. My fists are balled and my fingernails slicing red crescents into my palms. I won't say anything. I won't let them get to me. I will keep my silence. Dignity. How much of this can Maa take? How much has she taken already, in all these years? For her sake, I will hold my peace. I can't be a paper tiger and snarl now. I can't walk out with my mother. Where would we go?

Everyone else in the room is looking at everything else but me. At the false ceiling. False! How funny is that. Irony, it's called. At their fingers. At the box of barfi.

You could have cut the silence with a knife. One beat – two – three – twelve. And then Kushal steps in. He clears his throat and puts his hand on his mother's shoulder. 'Maa, let me say something. After all, he's our little brother.'

He looks at me. 'Sharad, no matter what happens, we are one family. We stick together. We make our decisions together. And for the common good. No one should feel hurt.'

I know where this is leading. That I, for the common good, should leave Tia.

'We have nothing against you and Tia.'

Huh?

'She means nothing to us, Sharad, only you do. You are our brother. And we have such big dreams for you. And right now, no girl fits into this picture. There is time enough for all that. Let me tell you something today. We would have told you this later, eventually, but with this unpleasantness and all…so best we discuss it now.'

I look up. New military manoeuvre? Attack from the flank?

Kushal goes on, 'You are the youngest in this family. And the smartest.'

Whaaaa? Did not see that coming. Is this finally, finally, an admission?

He carries on. 'We want you to study at the best college in the world and get the best degree you want. Business hasn't been thriving, but we'll manage the fees for you, don't worry about that.'

Is this happening? This is the kind of fantasy I've had all my life, from which I've woken up whooping. And now, one look at Maa's eager face tells me this is no fantasy. It. Is. Happening.

I can't help myself then. I break my vow of silence. 'You'd do that for me?'

'Of course. Hey, you're our baby.' He cuffs me on the back of my head.

Everyone's back to looking at me. It's like the ceiling has lifted, false or not, and the sky is open to this room, to me. 'Come on, time for a barfi,' one of my uncles suddenly lets out a celebratory shout and passes the box around.

'Wait!' And they wait. It's like pausing a video. Someone's hand holding up the box, someone's hand midway from box to mouth, someone's head half-turned. 'Wait,' I say. 'What do you want in return?'

Kushal shrugs. 'Why would we want anything in return? We are family. Come back home after your studies. Join the family business. That's all. We want the smartest brain in the family working for us.'

For us, he said.

Not *with* us.

AK

Back, after a day I had dreaded. Many tough moments, but I didn't crumble. I like how strong I'm becoming (and it's not about my biceps). It's even better to get home. Home's feeling a lot more like home nowadays. Weird, huh, especially since we're in danger of losing it. The court is attaching it or something, though our lawyer says he's whipping up a strong case. And we have nothing to fret about. Or at least, years before we need worry.

'Great,' says my mom. 'Years are great. In that many years, I can disappear too.' I look at her in shock, but she's got this wry smile on. Has everyone in my family had a sense of humour and have I been so huffed up with self-pity that I haven't even seen it? Seen them? They've just been Mom-Dad-Sis. Labels. Roles. Figures in a family photo. Not real people with sharp, or funny, edges.

Sure, you love your family. But liking them is a bonus.[33]

Sunshine, Silk and Simone are now perma-fixtures in my room. I've moved their basket in. And they seriously take my mind off – like – the serious stuff. Can watch them for ages – nipping and squabbling and warring over the same toy like they want to tear each other apart. And then they cuddle up and sleep on top of each other in the same basket. Family! Wow, am I learning stuff in leaps and bounds lately.

My mom handles the media and the police. Neo's already packed off the do-gooders sniffing around. Mom's told Jaggu Kaka that he can be with us for as long as he wants to be. And she got our family doc in to check him, just in case his frail old heart had not taken all these developments well. 'Frail? Stronger than my own,' said the doc. 'It will all be fine,' I told Jaggu Kaka. He pinched my chin in his fingers, like he did when I was six (yeah, and has done ever since). 'I know,' he said. 'You should believe that, Baba.'

This is not like everything just went away. My arms and ribs and neck and every other square inch thump and ache and scream every time I even turn around. Gonna be quite a while before it all goes away.

Neo hops into my room in the evenings, with a bowl of nuts or something. And we have these heart-to-heart chats that we should have had all our lives. Which always end in her laughing and me mad at her when I realize she's scamming me.

'Thanks, Neo, for dropping Alisha home,' I say this evening, while brushing out Silk's ears, and then broach a topic that's been boring into me. 'When have you got to go back to the US? College?'

'I've got time, don't worry your pea-brain. Why? You sick of me already?'

'No, I'm not.' I protest. 'I love having you here. And to myself. Dad always monopolized you earlier. You're his pet. You do everything right, unlike me. Studying, eating well, working out, keeping fit, taking an interest in the business. I know nothing about that. You're his sun, moon and stars.'

'Dad doesn't know me. The sun would stop shining if he did.' Neo pauses and gives me an unfathomable look.

'Can you keep a secret?' Another pause. 'You know my roomie, Max?'

Do I know Max? Ha! Max this and Max that and how they cook biryani and hike on weekends and... blyuk! Do I know Max? Ha!

'I'm in love with Max. Have been for the last two years. Love, love like we-want-to-get-married love. I just don't know how to tell Dad and Mom. But now Dad's gone, and Mom won't care.'

'Big secret! You're so stupid when you talk about him, we all know.' I yank at a knot on Silk's other ear and she yelps. 'Oops, sorry!'

Neo looks at me and says, 'I haven't told you the secret yet. Max is a girl. Maxine.'

At first, I just shrug it off. 'Huh! You're just conning me again.'

Neo grins at me. 'No. No, baby bro. Silly little silleeee baby brother. No. But the secret is what that makes me.'

I look at her. 'Like, seriously?'

She smiles. And nods. I stare at her and after a few Reallys and NoWays from me and a few Yeahs and OhYeahs from her, I throw my arms around her and laugh. 'Oh yes, you're so busted now. You're so going to tumble right off the Princess Throne.'

'Or maybe not. I think they've always known. Who knows! Who cares!' she says.

I lean my head against Neo's and we sit there laughing. 'There's only one boy I've ever loved,' she says, and squeezes me.

24

RUHI

I've never felt so alone. Frightened. Determined. Confused. Excited. Terrified. Helpless. Strong. Protective. Mature. Stupid.

I sit on my fluffy floral quilt and pull out an album, and another and another of my baby pictures, till I've got the whole pile of albums stacked around me. Keeping me safe. Back in my childhood.

Why was I in such a hurry to grow up? Why didn't anyone tell me it would be so tough?[34]

Mumma's got little captions for each photograph.

Showing my first baby tooth. Smiley Baby! (That's Mumma writing for me, of course. Like she could, even then, decide what was in my head.)

I am a week old today. Good morning, world!

Nanaji feeds me rice. I spit it out. Everyone laughs. I howl.

First day at school. I want to be a doctor.

Yay! Won the Best Student in class five. I want to be an astronaut.

Holiday in Shimla with Mumma-Papa. See my new hand-knitted sweater.

On my first bicycle. I cried till they bought it for me. I can now be like all the other girls.

Riding downhill – Papa running behind me.

In the hospital. Hairline fracture. Papa will never let me ride my bike again.

Thirteenth birthday party. I am a teen now. Cutting my Potter cake with all the girls in my class. All my friends.

I stop on that page. I feel so alone. I want to go back to the Potter cake, further back to the knitted sweater, and further back to spitting out my first grains of rice with Nanaji. I know I can't. For a start, Nanaji isn't even alive any more. I'm on my own.

I have dug myself into this pit and I'm going to have to pull myself out. Or pull Twilight in.

AK

Dad's sent a message. Through the lawyer. That he's fine. That he knows we are fine too. (How?) That he'd sort things out. That everything is being blown out of proportion. That he has not done anything wrong. That this is how business is. Shades of grey. That he had not run away with the people's money. That he'd just invested it in high-risk avenues. That is how business goes. Ups and downs. That he'd go to the court. That he'd fight for justice. (For himself? Not for those people, for sure.) That they would not be without a home. That he'd build what he'd promised to. That he always kept his promises. (Not true.) That we should not believe any of the media stories about him. That he couldn't get in touch with any of us because we would be followed, phone-tapped, spied on. That he would find a way to reach out soon. That we should be strong and have faith in him. That's the way business is. Good times and bad. ('That's marriage,' says Mom, 'he's mixing it up.') That we should remember all the good times we had. That we should remember how privileged we were. That we should not tell anyone anything. That we should give all the files in his shelves to the lawyer. That we should lock his room. That it is business as usual. That he's done nothing wrong. That Neo should study hard and take over the business soon. That she alone would understand. That's the way business is. Tough and tougher. That I should toughen up now. That I need to grow up. That I should look after Mom. (Mom and I do some excellent arching of eyebrows at each other.) That he is fine. That he is in a country where they wouldn't find him easily. ('With dancing girls in coconut shells and grass skirts,' says Mom). Not that he is hiding or needs to hide. That he has done nothing wrong. That he is fine. That there is no issue about money. That he has kept enough aside for a rainy day. That we would be fine too.

ALISHA

Back home. After school. After AK's sis dropped me. After Ruhi had already called my parents to tell them I was found, that I was okay, and that I'd been at school all night. Just that I'd fallen asleep after class. She left out the rest.

Back home. Without my phone. Without any trace of my make-up. Without any excuses. Open the door softly, Alisha. You want to avoid the disappointment in your father's eyes. Again. Just tiptoe into your room quietly without anyone noticing.

'Alisha? Is that you, child?'

And then my parents are throwing themselves at me, my father crushing my face into his white kurta that, I notice, is wrinkled for the first time ever. My mother trying to get her arms around me too. Moni shrieking over and over, 'Didi!' And from the corner of my eye, I can see her jumping up and down.

I lose track of what everyone is saying over one another. We were so worried. You're okay, no? God is great! We went to the police. We went to the hospital. You're hurt, not serious, no? We asked all your friends. You must be so tired. Ruhi said you fell asleep in school. Thank God! We couldn't sleep all night, calling and calling you. You want some halwa? I'll heat it up. Pizza – should we order your favourite? You want to bathe first? Coffee? Tea? Early dinner? Why are you crying, *beta*? Monisha, go buy some chocolate from the shop downstairs. I don't want to. I want to stay here with Didi. Sit, *beta*. Monisha, take her bag at least. Can't you see how tired she is. Don't cry. It's all okay now. You are home. What happened to your leg? Eat bread and jam. Here. I couldn't even go to office. Didi, you really want chocolate – I'll go get it. We were so frightened. Here, now eat. Don't worry now, eat and rest. We love you so much.

I don't deserve this. Especially not that last line. I eat though my throat is choking up. It's an effort. To send each mouthful scraping its way down. To eat through the curtain of tears. I eat. Everything they bring me. And they keep bringing it out. Hot food. Cold drinks.

For the first time in my life, I begin to see myself as lucky.

All this time, I wasn't being a star. I was being a victim. It hits me as smoothly as that. Thwack!

I used to swing upside down on the parallel bars in the playground gym as a kid.

And looking at things the other way around always made the difference.[35]

To be here. Exactly where I am. Funny or what? Hated this place all my life. Wanted to get out. Get out there. Be a star. And now, for now, there's nowhere else I want to be but here.

AK

My phone pings at the dinner table.

Mom scowls, like, why do I have a phone at the dinner table. And I return her look. Like, that's because we've never sat together at dinner time before.

I steal a peek at the message. And feel a shiver rip through me.

My face must have shown it because Mom says, 'What's wrong? Who's that?'

Neo says, 'Dad again?'

I say, 'No. Somewhere I gotta go.'

SHARAD

'I don't believe in taking right decisions,' I tell Maa, when we get back to our room, the barfi sitting heavy in my stomach, the weight of the decision even heavier.

Maa sits on the bed. It's her way of saying, Speak, she's listening.

'*I don't believe in taking right decisions. I take decisions and then make them right* – Ratan Tata.' I continue, 'Maa, I want to study at the best college in the world. And I'm grateful for the money your family, okay, okay – *our* family is ready to invest in me. But I can't sign away my entire future for that.'

I go on. 'I am going to tell Kushal Bhaiyya that. I don't know where I'll go, where I'll get a job, where that job will take me, or bring me back to. And maybe, some day, I'll come back and work in the family business. But I can't promise all that now. Not at this point.'

It is the most courageous thing I've done and the scariest. Willingly dashed my mother's hopes. I am terrified that she will faint or go on a hunger strike or something, and I will carry that guilt for the rest of my life.

'I'm sorry, Maa,' I say. 'If they still want to sponsor me despite that, I would be happy.'

I wait for her to say something – how disappointed she is in me – how she gave up everything for me. It's been the subtle underlying hum of all our conversations.

She nods.

'Okay,' she says.

I gulp. There's a catch. There's gotta be a catch. I watch her like the prey of a cuttlefish. Yes, they hypnotize their prey. Do not challenge an A-plus student on facts, okay?

Just that now I'm thrown off-balance. Confused. This is not how she's supposed to react. To take my insubordination so calmly. Where's the mega argument, the negotiation, the blackmail?

If it's gone through this far, let me push it further.

'I have something else to say. Another decision,' I point to Ratan Tata hopefully, like he's going to bail me out.

Maa nods again. 'Tia,' she says.

I gawk. Then recovering quickly, I say, 'Yes, Tia. I owe it to her to go and apologize for the way our family treated her. If she's okay with me, which obviously she won't be, because who in the world would sign on to get insulted by our lunatic family. Well, I'll just go talk to her, Maa. I don't care if she doesn't fit in here. She doesn't have to…'

Maa says, 'I know you will.'

This is totally the opposite of how it's supposed to be going. She's way too pliant. There must be a master-move coming up. Maybe the door will be shut and I will be locked into this house for the rest of my life. Maybe they're planning downstairs to drug me and tie me to my study chair. (Got to stop watching those videos.)

Maa is saying, 'I hoped we could change your mind. But I knew you'd do what you wanted to. You're exactly like –'

She pauses. And I look up sharply. Like my father? Is that what she's going to say? Tell me that I'm a deserter like my hated (in this house for sure) father? That I cared as little for anyone else's feelings?

'Like your mother. Like me.' Maa smiles. 'As stubborn.'

Maa gives me a box. It's an old shoebox. 'For Tia,' she says.

'Oh gawd! Maa, that's unbearably dramatic. You've been watching too many soaps. What is this – our heirloom jewels for her to have?' Though why family bling should be in an old shoebox beats me. I smell a scam.

I open it and see a whole lot of notes and cards and stuff. She's kept everything I ever drew or wrote – silly old poems and stick drawings of astronauts with gigantic heads and school essays that made it into the school mag, and all that.

'So she can get to know you better,' my mother says. Sharing my childhood is probably the toughest thing she could do. I don't know what to say, but she saves me the trouble. 'Tell her I want it back.'

My turn to nod.

I hold up the shoebox like a trophy.

'*Victorious warriors win first. And then go to war.* Sun Tzu.'

25

ALISHA

Is there, like, actually a happy ending? I've always refused to believe in one. I've invariably picked out books and movies that are dark, dystopian. Because, like, that's reality. The world is not made up of sugar-candy dreams. Not of people as vapid and smiley as Moni's pink stuffed toys. It's all sharp edges. See my knees, thighs, palms – see the scratches, the bruises. You don't get those in soft, fluffy, whipped-cream paradise.

But still.

Still. I'm here. Pulled back into this place where I've been all my life. With the people who sat with me all night through childhood fevers, the blackest of my teen lipsticks, the bluest of my teen moods, my threats of running away, my screaming that I hated them.

My eyes are drowsy, my room toasty warm, my stomach full. Too full.

I feel the cramps. The familiar sensation of lava pushing up. Bubbling up to my throat.

I rush to the bathroom. Slam the door shut behind me. Throw up into the toilet bowl. My body's betraying me this time. I don't want to. But it is what it is. I can't keep my food down.

I stay in here for half an hour, water running, tears streaming. I don't want to be like this any more. I don't want to be sick. I want to be as healthy as anyone else.

There, I said it. I want to be like anyone else. Not a star, Alisha? Just an anyone else? That could be an option. Normal people, who live in middle-class houses and drive old beat-up cars? It doesn't seem all that bad now.

Finally, I wash my face, dab it dry and step back out, into my room.

Moni stands there. She's been there all along. Waiting for me.

'I know, Didi,' she tells me with the seriousness of a thirteen-year-old in her eyes. 'I know what you do in there. I've known for some time now. How you stay thin. How you keep nothing inside you.'

My mouth is dry.

Moni continues, 'Didi, you're my hero. I want to be like you. Thin like you.'

I'm stunned at first, then furious. 'Don't you freakin' dare! Ever! Don't you even, like, think of doing this.'

She doesn't back down. 'Why not? I want to be a star like you.'

'Not like this. You can be anything you want to be. But not like this. Don't you ever do it!' I hiss at her. 'Never,

Moni, do you get me? It's not being beautiful. It's being sick. I'm sick. You are beautiful. Moni, never even try.' I'm blabbering now. What have I been doing to this person who is the most precious thing in the world to me?

She looks scared, but nods.

I grab her hand so tight that she winces and I place it on my head. 'Promise me. Swear on me.' I whisper through my streaming eyes, clenched teeth.

'Sure,' she whispers back.

I drag her by her hand into the living room where my parents are sitting and watching something on TV, a singing competition they never miss even if the pressure cooker whistles itself out.

I stand in between them and the glare of the TV screen, pulling Moni beside me. The way I used to as a child. To snitch on her. To say, Look, Moni ate the *chikki*. Look at her teeth, you can see the peanut bits. Open your mouth, Moni!

My parents look up at me.

It's been easy to roller-skate through life, pretending it's all about myself. Not that simple![36]

I may crash, but not into her. I can't let that happen to Moni.

And then I say the thing that I find the most difficult. What I never ever dreamt I'd say. But I will, because of my stupid li'l sis.

'I need help,' I say, clearly loudly. 'I want help. Please take me to that therapist. I want to start getting better and I can't on my own. Help me.'

There. Said it. Not that tough after all? But it is! T.O.U.G.H.! The toughest thing I've ever done.

My parents are beaming at me and nodding, senti and all that. My mother slides over on the sofa, and invites me to sit by her. We all watch a little girl in a yellow dress sing a song that sounds cutesy because she lisps through her missing front teeth. The judges go delirious clapping. My parents join in. Moni and I roll our eyes at each other. But it's not sarcastic. It's...you wouldn't get it.

My phone pings. I read the message and stand up. There's somewhere I need to go.

SHARAD

I'm here. Outside Tia's house.

It's taken all the guts I have. And then some. I'm trying to summon up some motivational quote. Zero zilch. Zero was invented by Aryabhata. There are more than a hundred million brain cells in my gut. Useless trivia. No inspirational words even floating by.

Tia lives on the first floor of a two-storey building. The ground floor has a store that sells medical equipment in bulk to hospitals. Great. Maybe I'll collapse and they can wheel me up on a trolley to see Tia. It's the way it would have happened in a movie.

The lights are on in their apartment. And there's noise. Some music. Something on TV? Or someone playing a guitar? What's going on? Whatever it is, I'm not invited. Clearly. Not welcome.

I need to charge myself up. Kickass quote, please happen. About courage, about taking the first step. The first step is the only way you'll know whether you're walking into dog poop. Author – me. I'm capable of many really bad quotes.

Happy Birthday! That's the song that's playing now, and a few voices belting it out. A birthday and she didn't tell me, didn't call me, didn't want me. I turn around to tiptoe away. Feeling defeated. Like an army withdrawing. Stealthily.

And then I trip. And yell as I hit the ground hard. And drop my shoebox. I scramble quickly on to all fours, trying to pick up as many fallen bits of paper as I can. Maa will slaughter me if I lose any. I sneak a wary glance up at the lit window and see a couple of heads pop out of it. Probably looking for the producer of that bloodcurdling scream. Now would be the perfect time to faint. Into a hole. Which should appear immediately, on call.

And into that window pops the backlit silhouette of a head I know so well, its curls spiralling all over.

'Sharad?' Tia calls out, more in disbelief than in Juliet-swooning tones.

In a few minutes, she's down, crawling with me in the gravel outside, picking up the papers to stuff back into my shoebox. I love her. I love that she's helping me pick up Maa's memorabilia without even knowing what it is. In fact, she's the one doing most of the picking up because I'm gazing dreamily at her.

In another few minutes, we're in her apartment. Her family is actually celebrating a birthday, that of her little brother. He's this hyper little minion in dungarees, jumping around, trying to burst all the balloons. There's a miniature dog that looks like a cat, which is fawning over me. The little sister, not to be outdone, bounces on my knee. Everyone seems to be wildly excited that I'm there. There is a cat. And is that a tortoise? I gawp. All in this crowded little room. It smells like what a home should smell like. Of dog, kids, of something baking? And then Tia's mom walks out of the kitchen, wiping her hands on her jeans.

She holds a hand out to me.

'I'm Sharad,' I manage to say without messing it up.

'I guessed – I've heard so much about you,' her mom smiles. She's got a wide, toothy smile.

She's heard so much about me. Me? I look at Tia, who shrugs.

So here I am, sitting on their sofa, eating cake, the dog on my lap now, and the little sister bitterly complaining to me about the birthday brother. I look at Tia again and I think of how she was treated by my family. And I choke.

She's looking at me too. 'It's okay,' she says.

I tell her I'm deeply sorry and I tell her every mushy thing I've heard in songs and movies. I don't really care that the sister, brother, not to mention the menagerie, are all listening in. I also tell her about Maa and the shoebox, the family business offer, the atrocious grades and the college plans, and how none of that really matters because my future is wherever a curly-haired girl is, if she still wants me.

She says she'll make up her mind in another twenty-five years, if I'm still around by then.

The cake begins to taste absolutely fabulous.

I want to be here forever. For the next twenty-five years, for fifty. And then my phone pings. When I see the message, I tell Tia I will see her tomorrow. And the day after. And the day after that. For the next few decades... yeah, yeah. But now, right now, I have to go.

26

RUHI

The school grounds at night, without the sunshine, the scattered lunch boxes, the flying basketballs, cricket bats, footballs, frisbees, the shrill screaming of primary school kids hurtling around like molecules out of control. No teachers to insist futilely on good behaviour and the lowering of voices. No voices at all. Just silence and shadows. Why is this place so dimly lit? Why haven't they repaired the break in the back wall? Was it all building up to this moment? For now? For me?

I look at the old familiar buildings around me. It feels like they're closing in on me now, casting long shadows. My heartbeat seem to echo through the deserted fields, corridors, stairwells.

I look at my phone for the hundredth time. Should I tell my parents? What if I don't go back home after this? I run away or...? I did message someone, just in case, you know...but there's been no reply.

I study the brick I've picked up from the pile near the hole in the back wall, waiting to be repaired some day.

Some day when something alarming enough happens for them to repair it. Like today.

I slip the brick into my backpack. It feels heavy. I can swing it out and I can hear the satisfying crunch it will make when it connects with a face that comes too close.

Can I really do that? Hit someone, keep hitting him till he drops? Is that self-defence? Or should I just run away and never come back. Go where? My mind is too rational to think of running away as the perfect answer to a multiple-choice question. How will I survive, eat, study? How will that make my parents feel? I'm a minor, how would I earn a living? How would I evade the police?

I don't know what I will do tonight. Do I give in to Twilight's trashy photo plans? Do I appeal to his sense of decency? Do I threaten to call the cops? Do I take a stand, call his bluff and tell him that I will not be blackmailed? Do I say that I don't care who knows, and it wasn't my fault?

But I do care. I can see faces. My mother's, my father's, my favourite teachers', schoolmates', neighbours'...I do care. But I've done nothing wrong. I'm the victim here. I'm brave, strong, educated. And I'm not going to play the helpless wilting victim any more. It ends here.

I walk to the centre of the basketball court. It has one high lamp presiding over it. The others have been switched off. It is the most brightly lit spot on the school grounds.

I look up at the terrace where I had seen Alisha spread her arms. Alisha has always been my role model.

Should I? Also? Go there? Do that? Even think that? It would be so much easier. No, of course not. Not in a million years.

But right now, I can't think of any way out.

It's 10 p.m. and though I got here early, he hasn't come. Maybe he won't. Maybe this will all go away. He will have a change of heart. He will discover his noble side. Good always wins. Every story ends with that moral: good always triumphs over evil.

'Hello, baby.'

A shadow detaches itself. Twilight walks out, with that shoulder-swaying swagger that I thought was so cool, and which makes me want to barf now.

'Great to see you. Been waiting so long. Verreh nice look!' He smiles at my stubbly head, my anxious face, like he thinks the world of me. He gives me hope. For a millisecond. Then he turns and calls over his shoulder, 'VC, she's ready, bro. Where are you?' A guy walks out behind him. I vaguely recognize him from that party, from the car out of which I flung myself – the headband guy. He looks shy, like we're meeting for coffee. He holds up his phone. 'Hi,' he shrugs. 'I'm the photographer.'

This is happening. What do I do?

Twilight is still a few feet away from me. He's pulling something out of his backpack. And I quickly shrug mine off as well. My hands sweating, I get a grip on the strap. It feels heavy.

He's pulled out a bottle. 'Here, have some, baby,' he says, still smiling. Silver eyes, silver teeth, I have this sense of déjà vu, of spinning back to when it all began. 'You liked it the first time around. Have a sip, come. You'll feel chilled out.'

He begins to walk towards me. His friend holds up his cell phone. The camera is on. The film has begun. The film starring, without my permission, me.

I tighten my grip on the backpack's strap. I've decided. I will go down fighting. He needs to know he can't prey on girls like me, who trust people. I'm not weak.

When he's a foot away, he holds out the bottle to me, towards my lips. I swing my bag around at his face. I want to crush it and knock out the silver teeth. However, I'm not built like a superhero. And my arm doesn't quite make the arc I imagine it will. The brick makes the bag lopsided, and although it swings up, it's not high enough. It hits his outstretched hand, and the bottle smashes to the ground.

Twilight looks surprised, and then a gleam flickers through his silver eyes. He lunges at my shoulders, effortlessly spins me around and shakes me like a shoe that sand has gotten into. He's hissing, furious, but I can't hear what he's saying. The buzz in my ears is too loud. I kick out like I've seen on TV. I hear my foot snap against his shin. And then he's swung me around and I fall to the ground. The basketball court is gravelly. But I feel no pain. Just terror. I scramble for something I can use to hit back, my hands clawing the rough ground. There's nothing.

No one. Nothing. I'm alone. I have to fight. I'm strong.

I prep myself to fight off his attack, but there's none. No fist, no body, no foot crashing into me. I look up to see Twilight and his friend have twisted around. There is someone they're looking at, who's limping in, someone with a ridiculously thick arm. Can it really be…it is! AK!

'Hey! You –!' Won't repeat what he called Twilight, not language my parents allow me to use. 'You want to pick on someone your size?'

Twilight looks dazed for a moment, then laughs. 'Who are you? And exactly what are you going to do? You look like you've been beaten up already. Happy to do it again if you want. Stay out of this, man!'

'How about me, then?' Someone else is walking out of the shadows. It's someone I've seen before. OMG, it's Niharika, AK's sister. She's got an even bigger swagger than Twilight has.

Twilight makes the mistake of laughing when she gets too close to him. He says, 'A girl? Really?' He shoves her away and turns towards me. And that's when she grabs his wrist and twists it backwards. He screams while she brings up her knee and slams it in between his legs. Ouch! He's dropping in agony now, and Niharika helps his collapse along with a punch I can hear from here. I want to whistle and applaud the way they do in movie theatres. I've got to get her to teach me these moves.

The photographer! I point at him to tell them that this is all being caught on video. I see him hurriedly backing away, still recording, though. And then there are more shadows, unlinking from the blackness around the buildings. More people blocking his escape.

I get to my feet and see faces I know. People from my class.

Alisha delicately extricates the cell phone from the wannabe-photographer's fingers and walks towards me. She winks at me. 'Evidence!' she says. I grin widely.

And then there's a whole lot of raised voices. Sharad has entered the grounds with the befuddled guard and the cops. Cops! Obviously, he'd be the one to think of that; his brain works in a crisis. Scratch that, his brain works all the time.

I look around at all the people around me. I had sent a message to AK, that was all, to tell him what I had decided to do, and what he should do the next day if I disappeared. He didn't wait until then. He just landed up. And made sure everyone else did too. They came to help me. Me. Little me. No. Scratch that. Strong, smart me. How could I have whined myself into a corner, thinking I was alone? I see people who have left their dinners and their beds and their cosy homes for me. My friends. MY. FRIENDS.

After Midnight

TIA

It's been four months since that night. I tagged along with Sharad, of course. You didn't think for a minute that I would stay back and miss all that drama, did you? You don't know me well enough, obviously.

Since those idiots are all high on life and all, let me fill you in on what's been up since then.

Neo went back to college and to Max. Her mom's going to stay a month with them, in fact. Apparently she said she wanted to see some Hollywood star she's had a crush on since she was young. She's been planning disguises to get into his high-walled, high-security house on a hill. Everyone likes Max. She's so fun! Jaggu Kaka sent her home-made sweets. She has only to get the dogs' blessings and then she's officially family.

Their dad is still a no-show. The courts have attached most of their assets to pay back those who had invested in the housing project he had scammed. Their lawyers have proved that the rest of the family had nothing to do with his shady dealings.

AK hasn't broken any new bones yet. Yet. He seems to have grown, like, a foot taller since then. AK's cute. Not half as cute as Sharad, though.

Alisha has started therapy. And hey, I love how she tells it. If you've got a broken nose, you go get it fixed. That's what she's doing. Just that. She had to be admitted into hospital for a while, for her eating disorder. She has put on a wee bit of flesh on those bones, so I'm guessing it's working out. And she's learning to play the flute. Spends hours at it. Some day, she's going to be topping the charts. Or not. I don't think she's doing it for that.

Ruhi told her parents about it all. It was tough. On her. On them. But there is no easy way out of everything. They don't baby her so much any more. She's growing her hair back. But this time, it's because she wants to. She says she wants it to grow longer than her little black skirt.

I've gone back to working part-time in the café. I managed to ace my exams too. Some day I'm going to be a doctor. 'Like me?' my mom asked. 'Better,' I grinned.

Sharad's got to this comfortable truce at home with his extended family. They did ask me to come over again. And again. We decided I wouldn't go. And then one day, my doorbell rang, and his Badass Badi Maa was at the door. She came in and sat on the creaky sofa (while my tortoise fixed her with an unblinking glare). My mom was nicer, she can melt ice with her smile, my mom. Anyhow, all that BBM wanted was to invite me over to their place. She said 'Please' like a dozen times. And so I went. They made a cake especially for me because

Sharad told them I like cake – and though it wasn't half as great as the ones my mom bakes, I said it was tasty. And that was that. A kinda happy that.

They say that we kids hit this tough phase when we're twelve years old or so, and it gets scary, confusing, from then on. The night gets darker and lonelier after twelve, right? That's what these are – the teens – the midnight years. But we all get through them, each in our own way, crushes, crashes et al.

On a video call, one random day, Ruhi said out of nowhere, 'I never thanked you guys for landing up that night. That dark, hopeless night. It made all the difference to know I'm not alone.'

Alisha added, 'No matter how dark the night, there's always a new day coming up.'

Sharad smiled. 'Give every day the chance to be the most beautiful day of your life.'

'Sharad!' the others laughed, 'You've grown so soppy, dude!'

'Blame Mark Twain – he said that,' he pointed at his wall. 'But you know who I'm saying it to.'

I said nothing, just grinned goofily.

AK added in his newly serious, responsible-sounding voice, 'There's always light at the end of the tunnel.'

Neo quipped, 'With your luck, that's probably an approaching train. Just don't break any more bones, baby bro!'

Have you ever – or perhaps sometimes – felt like Alisha, Sharad, Ruhi and AK? Do you have the same questions and thoughts in your head as they do? Here's where a psychologist dives into their feelings and queries – and yours.

TALK SPACE

The following pages have broad guidelines to understand feelings you may have in situations you may face. These are responses to the questions and issues raised by the teens in *The Midnight Years*. However, every individual has unique challenges and every circumstance is just that bit different, so if you need to, it's best to seek help in person from a qualified counsellor, psychologist or psychiatrist.

2

1. Who decides who's happening? Ever wondered?

Let's start with what makes a person cool or happening, according to you.

Typically, these are definitions that come from what your peer group aligns with: How popular is someone in the group? Does it depend on how many people want to hang out with them, perhaps because of the sense of confidence they exude, their ability to speak in a certain way, the way they dress, their ability to address difficult situations, the number of parties they get invited to, their prowess in extracurricular activities, their smartness? Some of them seem to have it all.

It is understandable and quite all right that you want to be part of the popular crowd. To have 'fun' and to be part of the 'fun set of people' does not change very much with age.

This need is just more augmented at the life stage at which you are. As part of your identity formation, you experience a need to be validated, to be accepted by your peers. This is a life stage that most of you and your peers are churning in together. The pressure to be 'cool' can be daunting. You feel that you 'should' have certain qualities and if you don't, you fear missing out on 'things that matter' or you begin to see yourself as less than others.

What is interesting is that this question has found an echo in you: Who decides who is happening?

The confusion or anxiety you feel in your body or mind – or both – could be indicative of your readiness to question the stereotypes of cool, to challenge someone else's authority to decide who or what is 'happening'. You are ready to define those terms for yourself – to 'individuate'.

2. She's so beautiful I can't breathe.

An intense feeling has overcome you, almost like you have been hit by a bolt of lightning. Romantic love or attraction is different from any other kind of love. It makes you feel instantly connected to another person – important, understood, secure.

What you may be experiencing when this happens for you is sexual attraction influenced by your own evaluations of physical attractiveness.

Deep parts of your brain get triggered easily and drive you emotionally. Increasing levels of testosterone and oestrogen, along with other hormones that are rushing through your body due to the fast-paced restructuring in your brain, influence how you experience other people –

with excitement, sexual curiosity, and a desire to form a relationship – a bond. Crushes happen easily.

Just the sight of someone you find attractive is enough for the endocrine system to flood your body with hormones that cause stress, happiness and a deep attachment to your romantic interest all at the same time! Nature provides this response, and your upbringing further accentuates and strengthens the natural chemical reactions based on the social messaging that's imprinted in your brain – from all the stories you've heard (or read) about love and intimacy from your social ecosystem.

This intense emotional and physical reaction can be overwhelming for you.

3

3. Ordinary is the worst thing I can be.

Is it really the 'worst' thing?

Ordinary to you may feel like you are a wallflower, and your need to be more than that is understandable.

If you are 'unordinary', you may feel more powerful, more special. In your social group, those who dress differently, party madly or lavishly, experiment with the forbidden, have the teacher's ear, hold positions of high visibility and/or seem to exude confidence or have panache, perhaps have an edge over others.

But 'unordinary' is not a formula to be replicated. What you deem 'unordinary' will be defined by the rules you set for yourself. Rules that reflect your attitude and belief about yourself.

Rest assured, no two people are the same.

While you are on your path to create your own unique differentiator – that which is 'unordinary' – it may be helpful to spotlight your strengths and not be tied down by the 'shoulds' in your life. 'Should' statements, such as 'I *should* be extraordinary' may leave you feeling like there is absolutely no room for anything else.

Is it really, absolutely, hundred per cent true that 'Ordinary is the worst thing YOU can be'?

4. If I can't stop hurting, let me hurt someone else.

You are hurting inside and looking for ways to alleviate that pain or smallness you feel right now. Confusion, anxiety, pain, inadequacy and other intense emotions you experience are part of the metamorphosis by which you are challenged while you try to find your place in the world.

To ease these difficult, painful emotions within yourself, you may sometimes feel the need to lash out at others. You think that your own distress will be resolved if you strike out at others. You hope that if you hit out at someone else you will be left feeling more powerful and adequate. Most times you are not aware that you are reacting to a sense of helplessness you feel in that moment – and so it becomes critical to cultivate habits in your life that will help you channelize that hurt/tension that everyday experiences may bring your way. If you could speak to a supportive family member, a sibling or a friend, it may help reduce the sense of continuing helplessness. Alternatively, cultivating habits around physical activities, such as exercising at a gym, running, engaging with a peer support group or volunteering, puts the brakes on reacting to the intensity of emotions you are feeling and buys you time to choose how you would like to respond in a safe manner – right through life.

4

5. Why do I reach boiling point in a microsecond?

You find yourself getting frustrated, losing your temper and before you know it, saying/doing things you don't really mean or will regret later.

At this stage in your physiological development, there is speedy rewiring and restructuring going on in your brain's neural networks – especially affecting the emotional seat of your brain (the amygdala) that sits within the older parts of your brain. That is why you receive anything that seems remotely threatening or fearful to your survival, with anger and other impulsive reactions. Your amygdala can be hijacked before you know it.

Your ability to reason and move towards judgement is clouded simply because the more sophisticated parts of your brain are still developing.

You're like a speeding car with faulty brakes.

If you have experienced this, then perhaps you could practise this exercise during calmer times:

- The Body Scan Exercise: Imagine you are moving an X-ray from the tips of your toes to the crown of your head. Ask yourself the question, 'What's happening in my toes?' Slowly moving upward, at each point note the feeling or sensations for yourself.

Gradually building the awareness of body sensations will help you pick up agitated sensations when you are in an anger-inducing situation. You can then pause to choose your response before you react.

This is one way to make sure those brakes work properly for you.

6. What's normal? Is a family that clashes like this on a daily basis normal? Or is it just mine?

Conflicts or fights are part of family life. They are the ways in which the various family members air their grievances and move towards resolution. Even the 'seemingly' happiest of families have conflicts or fights when members have strongly opposing views, values or beliefs. More often than not, one or more members of the family are held hostage to emotions when there is a fight – especially with those they may be closest to. Members have different ways of expressing their anger – withdrawing with the 'silent treatment'; ignoring someone; or talking in a loud, aggressive voice, in a disrespectful, patronizing or demeaning manner and/or even displaying physical aggression, such as banging doors or hitting out.

When fights, arguments, bickering, hostility or silence become the only way to communicate between members and no resolution is found, that could lead to an unhealthy family environment, fraught with anxiety. The connectedness and communication between members of the family become strained and the members of this family will tend to find other ways of coping with this anxiety. These alternative ways may be self-destructive habits. You could use this as an opportunity to communicate with your family – talk to at least one member whom you feel close to and trust – about what bothers you and what you would like to be different; or to cultivate self-nurturing habits, such as a hobby, journaling, eating healthy or volunteering at an NGO.

However, if there is room to have open, respectful communication and dialogue – where each member can speak and express their emotions without fear – even fights can foster deeper interconnectedness among family members.

5

7. Is everything either good or bad, black or white, true or false? Yes? Or no?

Oversimplifying things or experiences – into black or white, good/bad – helps us make categories in our social world. It allows us to make faster decisions. Our ancestors used this kind of thinking for survival.

However, in this new, progressive world, human behaviour has become more complex than just the need to ward off any harm or threat to survival. Each individual's behaviour is affected by a multitude of factors, such as the sociocultural context that one inhabits, one's family experiences, attitudes, beliefs, motives, intentions, aspirations, and a set of guiding principles or values all influenced by the variety of experiences in one's life growing up – along with various other biological factors.

Each person's life is unique to them. What may be right/good/white for one person may not necessarily be the same for another person. To insist on a universal morality in this situation is difficult and irrational.

The more honest question perhaps could be: Who defines what parameters are to be used? And how are 'good versus bad' and 'true versus false' defined, while keeping your own safety and security needs intact, and ensuring that everybody else's safety needs are not compromised either?

While you use your experiences to formulate these parameters, the golden rule would be that in your pursuit of what you define as 'your good', you be considerate and compassionate to others in your social milieu as well.

8. I'm guilty even before I do anything wrong.

Feeling guilty reflects your accepting accountability for your (real or imagined) thoughts, feelings or behaviour. A moderate amount of guilt is a healthy feeling. It's your way of navigating your behaviour in a manner that is acceptable for you and the society you live in. It helps you dip into your internal radar and make different choices the next time.

When you feel 'guilty even before you do anything wrong' and it is laced with fears and anxieties, inhibiting you from expressing your thoughts freely, then it can be an emotionally draining experience.

You may be mistakenly thinking that you are solely responsible for harming another person; or you feel obligated to make the other person happy, even if that goes against what you really want to do; or you may be exaggerating the consequences of your actions. All these reflect your inability to look logically at the situation.

Your guilt stems from your core beliefs, things you have been taught or those you have learnt from all the way back in your early childhood. As such they are meanings you assigned to experiences or messages you received in the past. Today these same experiences or messages can be looked at differently by you and assigned new meanings

– adjusted to minimize the guilt you feel and make revised decisions on how you would like to construct new beliefs that contribute to your personal growth.

6

9. Will I find perfect love if I don't look perfect?

How you look is a large part of how you construct your self-image, of how you think you will be accepted socially. It feeds into your self-esteem and ego identity, which are under construction right now. Perfectionism in looks is an ideal that's difficult to reach because:

a) while you're trying to attain that perfect ideal/model, your self-criticism is high and the bar keeps moving;
b) you're experiencing physical and hormonal changes at the onset of puberty; and
c) the norms in your peer group are fast changing (thank your social media.).

Therefore, your obsession over looks and equating your 'lovability' with looks result in even more anxiety.

10. You tell me not to take risks. Don't you trust me?

Trust is such a valuable and fragile commodity.

You are trying to become an independent person, and as part of this stage of your development, you tend to question all boundaries set by your parents/caregivers.

Also, the emotional, pleasure-seeking, risk-taking and instant-gratification part of your brain – the amygdala – is more developed than the thinking, logical, rational, decision-making part of your brain. That's why your judgements may be clouded. You are more than likely to make quick decisions without thinking through their consequences.

As an adolescent trying to be autonomous, you may not endorse your parents' or caregivers' authority, especially over your personal domain. While they are trying to minimize risk and pain for you based on their own past experience, you may question their ability to trust you.

So, while they hand-hold you without your permission, you could loosen the grip by collaborative negotiations. You could share accountability for your behaviour with your parents/caregivers while also acknowledging that the consequences of your decisions would affect not just you but your most significant relationships. The art of trade-off to get what you really want can be cultivated while you encourage them to trust you.

7

11. How does forever love start?

With the rapid changes that are going on in your body, these years are confusing and emotionally challenging.

As you try to establish your own unique sexual and gender identity, a romantic relationship can help you learn how to manage your emotions, offer companionship, develop a more mature identity and contribute to your own sense of worth. However, there is a high likelihood that your peer expectations and your need to belong in a social group can influence your decisions about your romantic partner. Navigating relationships at this age paves the way for future adult relationships as well.

So the honest answer to this question is – you don't know if it's forever love. It isn't a formula. Romantic relationships are a challenge at any age.

12. A no is a no is a no is a no is a no.

The need to explore and experiment is a part of your life stage.

However, the ability to say 'No' is a healthy step towards adulthood. As difficult as it may seem at this stage in your life (because you may be confused or fear social rejection), your sense of physical, emotional and mental safety and security depend on it.

This power of choice (yours) and the ability to communicate it (also yours) allow for personal boundaries to form. Personal boundaries, in turn, protect you from unwanted physical contact, emotional and mental harm (caused, for instance, by hurtful words or other people's negative judgements), discourage addictive/destructive behaviour and go on to foster healthier relationships with yourself and others in your social world.

You are then one big step closer to being independent, and safely so.

8

13. I'm ashamed of where I come from, and ashamed of being ashamed.

You've hit a developmental stage crisis. You are trying to be independent, build your identity, be socially accepted and popular. Although you are trying to detach yourself from your family and home, a large part of you is still interwoven with them. At this age, you also have heightened sensitivity about how others in your peer group perceive you, evaluate you and judge you. Confusion stems from how you see yourself vis-à-vis how you would like to be seen.

Shame is more painful than guilt. Shame is a deeper personal, inner experience – you see yourself, feel about yourself, judge yourself, as inadequate and unworthy.

To feel guilty is to feel remorse about thought, feeling or action (real or imagined).

So, question whether you are more confused/ disappointed and if you feel guilty about how you think and feel, rather than ashamed.

14. Does fate decide, or do I?

By definition, fatalism affects your belief about how much in control you can be in your circumstances. It is an indicator of how you view your own capabilities and strengths while making choices. It reflects who is in the driver's seat of your life – you, or an external force.

While you are experiencing yourself as an independent autonomous individual in your social world, your attitude, beliefs and resilience will decide how you navigate the turbulence that life may bring along with it. You could discuss and debate this with a family member you look up to or within your circle of friends to clarify your thinking.

9

15. It's weird how often other families seem better than your own.

When your family does not always respond sympathetically to your needs (physical or emotional) or does not meet your 'ideal requirements', your sense of safety and social security are threatened.

When you feel emotionally connected to your family and see your family as an anchor that may be demanding yet supportive and committed to your well-being, it is unlikely that other families seem better than your own.

As a teen, you crave autonomy and are building an identity separate from your family's – while also trying to manage various other changes going on for you. This is a tumultuous phase of change where both you and your parents are renegotiating the influence/transactions you have with each other.

The grass will always seem greener on the other side.

10

16. Lies aren't lies when they're just protecting a parent from the ugly truth.

There is research linking teenagers to lying for different motives (which include protecting someone's feelings, or not taking responsibility for breaking a rule).

This may be partly because of the changes that are happening in the brain at this stage and the fact that lying is associated with risk-taking behaviour. It may also be because you want to push the envelope with your parents to protect your privacy in an attempt to be independent of them.

What seems like an altruistic motive (an intention to spare *them* anxiety) to lie to your caregivers may come at a high cost in the long term, as you get deeply caught up in the fabrication, with resulting anxiety.

17. Home sweet home.

Home is that space which provides a secure, stable emotional base while you traverse the changes and development in your life. These positive connections, with support from family members, give you reassurance during these tough times. You can come back here to have open conversations, collaborative discussions and guidance that will facilitate your crossing over to adulthood.

Your home interactions are your primary training ground to learn socialization skills, negotiate relationships and develop your capacity to solve problems. It is a place of rest and recouping, and its members (they may include pets) provide you with the care you need as you engage, experience and gain mastery over yourself and your world.

While a house is a building that contains a home, the home is made of members who offer each other unconditional acceptance, a safe haven, a feedback loop and protection while you build your capabilities to meet the world as an adult.

11

18. I push away those who are closest to me. Why?

In an attempt to stay separate, independent and autonomous, most teens will pull away from their caregivers, especially parents and other significant people who are invested in their well-being. Pushing people away also happens when you feel threatened, perhaps because your expectations (from yourself or others) are not met, or when you feel it's nearly impossible to make the healthy choices that you know you must make.

When your own desires are unmet and your anxiety is high, pulling away from those people who make you feel loved and accepted is your way of taking care of yourself. You are not in a place of readiness to address the anxiety even when those closest to you reach out to support you. You are afraid to show your vulnerability.

19. Binge-eat. Binge-purge. Binge-sleep. Am I trying to get something out of the food, or lose myself in it?

'Binge eating' is rapidly eating food in much larger quantities than most people would, at least three times a week over a month, and be left feeling uncomfortably full. It's very different from succumbing to temptations once in a way.

When it is repeated frequently and accompanied by dark thoughts related to body image, emotional pain, guilt, anxiety, low self-esteem and/or depressive symptoms, it is considered problematic.

Like most addictive behaviours, problematic 'binge' behaviours may be an escape from difficult feelings and traumatic situations, or even because of a biological imbalance in your body. It is time to ask for support. Professional intervention may be necessary for you to navigate out of this challenging experience.

12

20. I've deleted me.

According to Erik Erikson (the father of psychosocial development – he theorises about stages in the development of an individual's personality), the main social task of the adolescent is the search for a unique identity – the ability to answer the question: 'Who am I?'

The mind is inundated with such thoughts at this life stage.

While you seek an answer to who you are, who you want to be, and how you would like your family and peers to see you, you experiment with different identities, perhaps, in different situations. There may be one mask you put on for your friends, another for authority figures, a third for a romantic interest, but no mask at all where you feel you will be safest. There will be times when you perceive yourself in a certain way, but those closest to you may see something different.

However, you are not clearly committed to any of the different identities you try, and this may keep changing. It can leave you feeling confused, exhausted and/or emotionally overwhelmed.

Finding that one person whom you can speak to may help ease your emotional exhaustion.

21. He's the bad guy, right? Always has been. Never nice. Ever. People can't be both.

How you view a relationship, or an experience, is influenced by similar events from the past. You weave these events that have occurred over a period into a particular sequence to create a story that seems meaningful for you.

When you experience a particular person in a certain way over a period, you categorize him or her, build a belief and then look for evidence to feed into that belief. You are at an age where you tend to have an exaggerated reading of the other person's expressions or experience of you. Overgeneralization and judgement biases are an outcome of this.

You are at the neuro-socio developmental stage where your higher order cognition/thinking is forming. You now have the ability to question extensively – think and reason systematically about other possibilities, be aware and understand your own thoughts and emotions – as also think about others' perspectives.

When your assumptions or beliefs are challenged with new evidence, you raise questions about your own beliefs. You feel uncomfortable and may choose to stay within your comfort zone of old beliefs; or after much internal debate, you may be ready to formulate a new one.

It may be helpful for you to journal your thoughts to reduce the intensity of the disturbing feelings that come up for you, access more rational thoughts and get more clarity about decisions/choices you want to make. With the different apps available on your phone, journaling can be your easily accessible, confidential buddy, available anywhere, anytime, and just a fingertip away.

13

22. Love's overhyped. It's just a marketing gimmick. I'm not going to fall for it.

At this stage in your developmental process, an initial rush of chemical changes in your body when you see an attractive person can often be mistaken for love.

When there is a consistent need to be with this person over a long period of time, it requires room to share your vulnerabilities, care about each other's expectations, accommodate the other person's needs as much as yours, and an abundance of trust in building the 'we' in the relationship. Commitments come with many challenges.

When you are negotiating your own physiological and emotional changes, it may be difficult for you to have the bandwidth to accommodate another person's expectations and needs. You may rationalize it away as being too 'smart' to fall in love, but in truth, it's just simpler to focus on reconciling the 'I' rather than the 'We'.

When you have a tighter grasp on who you are, more confidence in your identity, a better alignment between how you see yourself and how the world sees you – and this extends to who each of you is in the relationship – then together you can build an even stronger and deeper 'We' in the relationship.

14

23. How can someone who's been knocked down so badly still bounce back? Am I still talking about her? Or me?

The ability to bounce back is resilience. Simply put, it is the ability to overcome intense negative emotions, adapt and grow in a healthy way after facing adversity.

Sadness and grief will most certainly accompany any crisis, but the inherent strengths that each of us has – such as humour, people skills, sports skills, a helpful nature, connectedness to a family member or friend, writing or other creative ability, and so on – can be used as tools to move from that place.

Perhaps the questions to ask when faced with adversity would be:

1. Is it absolutely, hundred per cent true that this is an insurmountable challenge?
2. What parts of my life/me have not been knocked down by this?

When you notice the ability of another person coping with what seems to be a rather difficult situation, it may be time to also check and reflect on your own sense of control over your own actions and their consequences.

15

24. Choices. Choices. It all boils down to choices.

Granted – on the one hand, you are now more at risk of making emotionally driven decisions that promise instant rewards (mainly because of the age-related rapid neurological changes); on the other hand, you are also developing your higher-order thinking abilities, for example, to understand how other people may think, feel or have different perspectives, and the various possibilities or outcomes of your actions. You are in a place of readiness to do a cost-benefit analysis of possible outcomes for long-term benefits. Which means you are now capable of looking ahead and understanding what you might gain and what you might lose – not just immediately, or in the next week or month, but in a few or more years – by making a certain decision.

It all boils down to putting the brakes on, controlling impulses, and oiling your rational reasoning ability to weigh the pros and cons of the choices you make. Doing a 'fact check' with a pen and paper, a journal of any sort or even using a sounding board – perhaps a mentor or a friend – may be helpful here.

16

25. When I don't want to be my father any more.

As a child growing up, you saw your mother and father (and/or significant caregivers) as providers for your physiological needs as well as your need for love and belonging. You looked up to them, adored them and depended on them to validate you and take care of your basic needs.

As a teen, you begin to discern flaws and imperfections in them. Your judgement of them is harsher and more critical. This is not surprising, simply because you want to be separate from them and autonomously explore your world. Yet, somewhere, you need them as safe places to come back to, to hold you securely, while you manage all the new confusing experiences that this stage of life brings your way.

If you come upon new critical information about a parent or significant person (someone you would have liked to emulate or put on a high pedestal) that shows them as having frailties, failures or incompetencies, it leaves you feeling stressed. Continuing to accept this parent/caregiver, whom you previously idolized, will become an emotionally turbulent experience.

In an attempt to separate from this person, you may need to reassess which of your current beliefs and values are aligned, and which you would like to change and/

or keep different from theirs. Talk to someone outside your ecosystem to achieve this clarity. This could be a mentor or a mental health professional – someone you trust and who you feel gives you a safe space to talk through your challenging thoughts.

17

26. Breaking out of a cocoon hurts. But I still need to. I need to flex my own wings now.

Growing up in the safety and security of your parents' home as a child was not difficult.

As a child who has been coexisting with family and other important people in a harmonious way, aligning with the expectations that everyone has of you – without rocking the boat – was natural for you.

However, as a teen you want to strive for independence, you have a natural need for autonomy, creating your own unique identity – everything about your family that was acceptable before is now perceived in a new light with new eyes. Your inner frustrations may keep building up as you want to push the boundaries of this safe, nurturing space to allow for your own voice to emerge.

You are deciding to take up a hard challenge (perhaps injuring a valued relationship) in order to grow and create a different identity for yourself. It can be painful also because it involves constantly wanting to find a way to balance being different from your family members – especially your parents – and yet expect to have them align with you always.

With respectful, consistent and open conversations with all the stakeholders in your cocoon – which means all those around you who have a part to play in this cocoon – the transition to flexing your own wings will become easier.

27. So much I want to say and I can't.

Your words are stuck in your throat. You are perhaps afraid of what the other person may think or feel about what you say, or perhaps you do not feel ready enough to share what's going on for you. It's simply uncomfortable.

Our brain has an age-old mechanism to respond to any situation of threat in a split second – it was a survival skill that our ancestors benefited from.

These hardwired natural stress responses are automatic reflexes to real threats, or even when they are not really needed, they are triggered by any situation that may be even remotely scary and outside of our control. One way of responding to any stress situation is similar to the sensation of freezing: wanting to say or do something, but not having the ability to do so at that moment.

Counting your breath while you inhale and exhale through your nostrils is one of the most effective tools to help that stress response pass.

19

28. Big boys don't cry, remember?

The messages we receive from our family and society feed into the beliefs and perceptions we form.

Some of the messages that get drummed into boys when they are growing up is that 'boys don't cry' or 'be a man' or 'don't be a sissy'. This is what is termed 'gender stereotyping'. Traditional masculinity in our culture encourages boys to want to be seen as tough, aggressive, domineering and stoic, while girls are generally expected to be more expressive, weak, vulnerable and emotional.

As a teen going through rapid changes in every aspect of your life, you may also have an exaggerated sense of how other people, or an imaginary audience, may be constantly thinking about and judging you.

If you are born male, masking or repressing your emotions to align with the traditional stereotyping may be a fairly painful and isolating experience especially in challenging times, while sharing with someone you can trust will lessen the intensity of your experience when you make a choice to challenge these traditional stereotypes.

29. When the only light I ever saw at the end of the tunnel, turned off.

When you feel like something you've been struggling with is going to be easier to manage and you feel motivated enough to believe that you can work through it, you experience a new sense of strength, a purpose for your life and insight into your own inner capabilities.

Then when the catalyst or the reason you felt motivated by goes away, a sense of sadness, feeling let down, 'stuckness' or even hopelessness sets in.

The sense of agency, the sense of being able to act and make a difference to the situation that you had a glimpse of when there was 'the light at the end of the tunnel' – the insight that you had – this reservoir of strength is still within you. And it's what you need to recognize, tap into and anchor on, even if the light of hope may at this point seem to be turned off. The disappointment will wear off, but that inner core of strength will remain with you in the long run.

20

30. I don't know how to get myself out of this whirlpool.

When you feel stuck in a difficult situation, you feel like you are drowning and being sucked in further, and there is no way out of it. You are threatened. Your survival instincts kick in automatically.

Your body will naturally respond to what you experience as threats with the age-old mechanism of survival – which may be either fight, flight, freeze or fawn response – the emergency mode. In such a situation, you might want to respond in different ways: with aggression (fight); running away by engaging in obsessive-compulsive activity such as too much smoking, gymming, cleaning, continuous boredom, even not being able to sit still (flight); daydream/sleep a lot or watch shows in a loop (freeze); indulge in people-pleasing to avoid conflict (fawn); or a combination of two or more of these.

Your 'go to' survival response to the threat will be unique to you.

In such times, you cannot access your thinking easily. You experience yourself as incapable of getting out of that situation. It can be an emotionally overwhelming experience.

However, in every whirlpool, there is always a way out that someone outside of it can see and guide you to safety. Much like the challenge you find yourself stuck in. Once you recognize or become aware that you are feeling helpless or stuck, when the thought 'I don't know what to do' comes up – it's time to reach out for support. A good choice would be to turn to a responsible adult you trust to guide you out of it.

22

31. With the mask off, with the wings off, with the crown off...am I still worth liking?

When you feel forced to drop your social mask that empowered you all along and reveal the real you, you can become apprehensive and find it almost daunting. You are taking a risk. When your need to be seen in a certain way is challenged by how you really see and experience yourself, questions about your likeability and your sense of worth will raise their self-critical heads.

Am I still worth liking if I show my real self to my world?

The answer to this lies in identifying and acknowledging those parts of you that you like, for example – specific skills that you have, physical features, your problem-solving efforts, your ability to help others, and what may even seem like the tiniest, most irrelevant feature to you.

How okay and compassionate you are with yourself when you judge your 'imperfections' will decide this answer.

Behind that mask is a unique individual. It's okay to embrace this distinctive differentiator that marks your identity.

32. At some point, you stop blaming the world, and start doing something about it.

Although right now you are naturally inclined to behave instinctively from your emotional self, you are also at the threshold of developing and sharpening your thinking brain. By developing the ability to regulate your emotions and making systematically thought-out decisions, you are stepping closer to being the curator of your life ahead. This is no easy task since you are at a very turbulent developmental stage of your life.

When you see yourself as being competent to make conscious choices and engage in actions to solve problems while also being accountable for your decisions, you are demonstrating healthy autonomous/independent behaviour. You are the captain of your ship while you navigate through an often stormy sea.

23

33. Sure, you love your family. But liking them is a bonus.

You love your family – it seems like the most natural thing for you.

But liking them/specific members is to acknowledge and accept that they are also imperfect individuals with traits that may annoy and irk you, that they will frustrate you, embarrass you, disappoint your expectations of them, and have strengths and weaknesses, or behave in ways that are hurtful to you. Or just that they think differently to you. Yet there is a sense of closeness and commitment you share with them because you sense their unconditional acceptance, attachment and a sense of responsibility for your well-being. They are different from you, yet a part of you.

Although society emphasizes otherwise, and it seems like a taboo – it's okay not to like certain traits or value systems that you cannot align with in some family members. Sometimes, just letting them know what's not okay with you and why it's not okay may help them grow to be the best version of themselves. Of course, test for readiness to share this.

24

34. Why was I in such a hurry to grow up? Why didn't anyone tell me it would be so tough?

You are moving from the safe haven of parents/caregivers making decisions for you and accepting accountability for what you do – to owning your own decisions and actions. You have your own thoughts independent of their views and beliefs about how you 'should' decide and behave. Sometimes you respond to these conflicts with rebellion, sometimes with compliance, and sometimes you have the ability to negotiate/transact and find a middle ground.

As you experiment with this new-found ability to have views and opinions, think objectively and behave in an independent, autonomous manner, you are met with difficult choices to be made, confusing thoughts and anxiety. It may be the right time for you to start keeping a journal as a tool. It's where you write down your innermost thoughts, or whatever it is that's on top of your mind, even discomforting sensations in your body, challenges facing you, moments of joy, anger or sadness…

Your journal can become:

1. Your non-judgemental sounding board, your safe sharing space – your secret buddy.
2. A confidential place where you can write, draw, or create a word collage about your thoughts, feelings and behaviour with honesty.
3. A space to alleviate your disturbing feelings – putting it all outside of you, writing it down, allows the intensity of that experience to reduce.
4. A feedback system that weighs the pros and cons of the choices you may want to make.
5. Your negative thinking or behaviour pattern tracker that helps you identify triggers and helps you manage them.
6. A place to pause and regain control over your emotions.
7. A value-add you give yourself to build your emotional wellness and take charge of your life healthily.

With awareness, mindfulness and consistent practice you can develop the rational thinking part of your brain. The carrot on the stick 'to grow up' would be the sense of autonomy and independence that tantalized you. With autonomy and independence comes responsibility, which is an integral part of being an adult.

35. And looking at things the other way around always made the difference.

It is like the adage: 'Can you see the glass half empty or half full?'. There is always more than one way of looking at an experience.

When you are in a place of readiness and feel supported, often after experiencing the initial disappointment, anger, frustration or even sadness in a given situation, you will have the strength to access those parts of your thought processes that are now more developed to think objectively about situations – from different perspectives.

How you interpret or give meaning to an experience in relation to you will trigger certain hormonal reactions in your body as part of the rapid physiological and neurological changes you are undergoing. These can influence what you name as feelings. Your behaviour is an output of these feelings.

And looking at things the other way around always makes a difference because it will give you access to choices that you may otherwise not have thought of. You may want to enlist a friend, or another valuable person who is outside your situation, to support you through this. Or even (if you feel ready) perhaps ask the questions for yourself:

1. Is it hundred per cent true that my interpretation of this is right? Could it be different?
2. How is this experience going to help me grow to be the best version of myself?

25

36. It's been easy to roller-skate through life, pretending it's all about myself. Not that simple!

The development of the 'self' as a separate, independent and unique personality is an ongoing process from birth, but it is particularly critical when you reach your teens. Your absorption with yourself is your attempt to integrate different parts of your physical and emotional self to create your unique identity or personality.

When you begin to take cognizance of other people's thoughts and feelings, and their perspectives, and respond to them effectively, not only are you building your social intelligence, but you are also moving a step closer to becoming emotionally intelligent and making healthy connections with yourself – and others.

Me reflects back as We, which is an integral part of wellness. While you develop your own identity, your peers and other valued people in your life act as feedback mechanisms to how you see yourself. You realize that you're not alone, that what you choose has a ripple effect, and what anyone else chooses also comes back to wash over you.

You step into adulthood.

Acknowledgements

This book took over five years to create. It was debated over, defragged, abandoned, rewritten. Again and again. We concluded that it was a story that could not be written. Then once again, we wrote it.

Vatsala Kaul Bannerjee of Hachette India spotted the glimmer in *The Midnight Years*. The book owes much to her passion, and her unwillingness to let a single line go unattended. Nimisha Chandel designed countless (we actually did stop counting) covers to arrive at one that told this story. Mita Kapur of Siyahi has been a guardian in more ways than one.

We thank our beta readers – Rohini Mehta, Maitreya Unni, Neel Nair, Aliya Ramachandran and Sayonee Banerjee – for their hard-hitting feedback. They made sure the book spoke as them, to them.

Always invisible but immeasurable is the support of our family and friends, who know when to help, when to just listen – and when to make their own dinners.

To those of you going through *The Midnight Years*, we hope this book makes a little more sense of the blackest times, asks your questions and gives you enough ammo to find your answers.

Notes to myself

Notes to myself